Don't Fall for the Billionaire Collection

Hana York

Pink Pop Publishing

Don't Fall for the Billionaire Collection

(Don't Fall for the Billionaire Books 1-3)

www.HanaYork.com

Contents

Hating Mr. Wentworth

A Flirty Enemies-to-Lovers Romcom Between the Billionaire CEO She Swore to Hate and the Woman He Can't Resist

Hana York

Pink Pop Publishing

Hating Mr. Wentworth

(Don't Fall for the Billionaire Book 1)

Copyright © 2025 by Hana York

www.HanaYork.com

Contents

Chapter One

LIZ

EVEN HIS NAME MADE my eye twitch.

Billy Wentworth the Third.

What self-respecting adult still went by *Billy*? Was *Trip* already taken?

I glared at the subject line in my inbox like it had personally insulted me:

Company Leadership Transition – CEO Introduction

The body of the email was bland corporate nonsense—vision, innovation, synergy—but the real message was clear: William Wentworth had passed the baton to his son.

And that meant my future now rested in the hands of some overprivileged, beer-pong-playing, ultimate-frisbee-throwing trust fund baby.

I scrolled past the glowing list of Billy's so-called accomplishments, which read less like a résumé and more like a LinkedIn fantasy crafted by overpaid PR elves. A European business school. "Strategic entrepreneurial ventures" (sure thing). A background in logistics, which probably meant *"my assistant booked all my flights."*

I was still scowling at the screen when a voice floated in from the doorway.

"So, how's it feel knowing our fate now rests in the hands of a guy who probably calls his buddies 'bro' unironically?"

I looked up.

Mia—best friend, product designer, chaos goblin—leaned against the doorframe, smirking. Sketchpad under one arm, pencil stabbed through her bun like a weapon.

I slumped back in my chair. "Infuriating. I work my ass off, and now Mr. Trust Fund with a private jet gets to decide if I'm worth keeping."

"He went to business school in Europe," she said, strolling in and dropping into the chair across from me. "Which means he probably spent three years drinking overpriced espresso and calling it networking."

I snapped my laptop shut. "I've spent five years building this portfolio. Five years of skipped holidays and writing pitches in parking lots. And now some billionaire baby rolls in to 'evaluate' me like I'm a line item."

"Rumor is he's hot, at least."

I made a face. "I don't care if he looks like a Hemsworth and smells like fresh cinnamon rolls. I don't trust anyone handed that much money and power."

"No argument. But if he *does* look like a Hemsworth... maybe you flirt your way into a raise."

I groaned. "If I have to flirt to keep my job, I'm quitting and opening a waffle truck."

Mia lit up. "Do I get equity?"

"You're COO and Chief of Toppings."

"Perfect. I've been dying to test my s'mores waffle."

The corner of my mouth twitched. But then reality crept back in.

There was one glaring issue with my credentials I couldn't fix: the missing degree on my résumé. The one I should've had—if it weren't for the Bradley Situation.

The one thing *Billy* might notice.

My stomach turned. I straightened. "Whatever. I'll do what I always do—work twice as hard and leave zero room for doubt. If he wants to fire me, he'll have to actually find a reason."

Mia grinned. "And if he does, we'll key his yacht."

I laughed. "You think he has a yacht?"

"Billionaire playboy? It's practically issued at birth."

I leaned back in my chair, the humor fading.

I didn't need to meet him to know exactly who he was. Rich. Polished. Entitled.

The kind of man who always came out on top—while girls like me were left cleaning up the mess.

"God, I hate him already." I muttered.

BRETT

I'd been at the office for less than an hour and already wanted a drink.

The conference room smelled like burnt coffee and desperation. A dozen executives sat stiffly around the table, faces split between forced enthusiasm and quiet panic. They wanted to impress me.

More accurately, they wanted to keep their jobs.

Couldn't blame them. My father had run this company into the ground, and now I was the one tasked with dragging it out of its financial grave. That meant figuring out who was actually pulling their weight—and who was just here for the catered lunches and quarterly bonuses.

An older exec leaned forward, clasping his hands like we were about to exchange state secrets.

"We're all eager to hear your vision, Billy. Where do you see the company in five years?"

"Brett," I corrected smoothly.

He blinked. "That's what I said... Brett."

"No, you didn't." I kept my voice even, though this was the *third* time someone had called me Billy since I walked in.

My legal name might be William Wentworth III, but I'd gone by Brett since college.

The nickname 'Billy' was my dad's idea of legacy.

And it wasn't one I planned to inherit.

The entire table shifted uncomfortably. I could practically hear the internal Post-Its being stuck to their brains: Not Billy. Brett. Do not screw this up!

And then—

A snort.

Quiet. Sharp. Definitely not imaginary.

My gaze locked on the source.

Blonde curls. Blue eyes. Curves that made my focus wobble.

She didn't look away. Didn't apologize. Just lifted one perfectly arched brow like I was wasting her time.

I didn't know who she was, but I knew exactly what that look meant.

She'd already written me off.

Another rich boy in a tailored suit who thinks "work ethic" is a brunch spot.

One look and I knew—she already had a nickname for me, and I wasn't going to like it.

I looked away first.

Not because I was rattled. Definitely not.

It would take more than a curvy blonde with attitude and a glare sharp enough to draw blood to shake me.

I just had a meeting to run. That was all.

Totally professional.

Totally unaffected.

I straightened my tie. "As for your question? It's simple. We're going to stop hemorrhaging money and start innovating again."

I let the words settle. Felt the collective pulse in the room stall.

"Bright Spark used to lead the industry in educational play. Now we're recycling the same stale ideas while our competitors eat our lunch."

Silence.

Not passive. Not polite.

Heavy. Weighted. Like everyone was trying not to look guilty.

A few executives glanced down at their folders—probably filled with the exact recycled trash I was talking about.

"Over the next two weeks, I'll be meeting with each department. Come prepared with data, not excuses."

I stood and buttoned my jacket.

"Meeting adjourned."

Chapter Two

BRETT

As THE ROOM CLEARED, I noticed the blonde lingering.

She moved slowly—deliberately—like she was waiting to pounce.

Great. Exactly what I needed before my first coffee had fully kicked in.

"Something on your mind?" I asked once it was just the two of us.

She looked up, eyes locking with mine. Cool. Unflinching. Blue as hell.

"Not at all, *Brett*."

The way she said my name dripped with sarcasm.

"You disagree with something I said?" I asked, more curious than I should've been. Most employees were still walking on eggshells. She looked like the kind of woman who'd argue with you, win, and still make you wish she hadn't walked away.

She tilted her head slightly, eyeing me like I was something unpleasant clinging to the bottom of her shoe.

"Nope. Just fascinated by how confidently you talk about innovation for someone who's been here, what—five minutes?"

Ah. So that's how this was going to go.

"I did my homework," I said, keeping my tone even. "And if my confidence bothers you, the next few weeks might be rough."

Her mouth twitched.

"Good thing I have a high tolerance for mansplaining," she said sweetly.

Then she smiled—the kind of smile that dared me to keep talking so she could shred me again.

I should've walked away.

I didn't.

Instead, I crossed my arms and leaned casually against the table—because, for some reason, I suddenly wanted to get a rise out of her.

"Should I be flattered, or are you always this hostile before noon?"

"Depends on the level of entitlement I'm dealing with before my second coffee."

That one landed.

I straightened slightly. "So you've already decided I'm an overpaid idiot with no clue what I'm doing?"

"Your words, not mine," she said with a shrug, gathering her folder.

I couldn't help it—I laughed. She was refreshingly honest. Everyone else in this building was either kissing my ass or walking on eggshells. This woman looked like she'd rather eat glass than pretend to be impressed by my last name.

Her eyes narrowed at my laugh, like I'd just failed some test.

"I'm glad you find this entertaining," she said. "Some of us have actual work to do."

"And you are…?" I asked, realizing I still didn't know her name.

She straightened to her full height—which wasn't much, even in those heels that made her legs look endless.

"Elizabeth Bentley, Senior Account Executive." She didn't offer her hand. "Most people call me Liz."

"Liz," I repeated, testing the name. It suited her. Short, sharp, no room for bullshit. "I've heard good things about your work."

She blinked, thrown for a half-second before her shields went back up. "From whom, exactly? You've been CEO for all of twenty minutes."

"Quarterly reports. Client retention data. Your name came up in my research." I wasn't lying. I'd spent weeks poring over every file, every report, every piece of data I could get my hands on. "You consistently outperform every other account executive."

Her chin lifted slightly. "I know."

She tucked the folder under her arm and turned toward the door, pausing just long enough to toss over her shoulder, "Well," she said with a bright, fake smile. "Welcome to Bright Spark, *Brett*. Can't wait to see your leadership in action."

God, she was impossible. All sharp edges and stubborn pride, clearly determined to hate me on principle.

So why the hell was I enjoying this?

Why was I still standing there, thinking about the way she said my name—like it was a curse and a dare wrapped in one?

This woman?

She was going to be a problem.

And I couldn't wait.

LIZ

I stormed into Mia's workspace without knocking—which was fine because she never knocked on mine either.

Her desk was a disaster zone of sketches, clay molds, and three different coffee cups in various stages of abandonment. She was hunched over her sketchpad, completely absorbed—until she looked up and caught sight of my face.

"Uh-oh," she said immediately. "Who pissed you off this time?"

"That would be Billy," I said sweetly. "I mean—*Brett*. Apparently, we're all supposed to pretend he's not a third-generation billionaire baby now that he's using his *'Serious Adult Name'.*" I added air quotes for emphasis.

Mia's eyebrows rose. "So? Was he as much of a douchebag as you imagined?"

"Worse. So much worse." I dropped into the chair across from her with a dramatic sigh. "He looked like the kind of guy who'd roll in from a yacht party—six-foot-four, broad shoulders, obnoxiously perfect brown hair, artfully tousled like he'd just woken up from a nap in a private jet."

Mia made a face. "Ew. So, infuriatingly hot?"

"Unfortunately, yes," I grumbled. "And he had the nerve to leave the top button of his shirt undone, like full professionalism was just a suggestion. Add that to the tailored navy suit, the smug look, and the tie he probably loosened for effect, and it's practically a walking billboard. One that says: 'I inherited this company and a yacht'."

"You sound... flustered."

"I'm furious," I corrected.

Mia raised an eyebrow but said nothing.

"He thinks he's clever," I said, gesturing wildly like I was presenting closing arguments on *Law & Order: CEO Unit*. "All calm and smug, with his rolled-up sleeves and his 'I'm not like other billionaires' energy."

Mia's head snapped up, eyes wide. "Did he actually say that?"

"No," I snapped. "But he radiates it. Like he thinks because he doesn't wear a Rolex or say 'synergy' every five minutes, we'll all forget his last name is Wentworth."

And then there was the way he looked at me—deep brown eyes fixed on mine, like I was a puzzle he was already bored of solving. And the way he said my name? Slow. Smug. Like he was rolling it around in his mouth just to see how it tasted.

Mia flipped her pencil and made a minor correction on her sketchpad. "Did you tell him that?"

"Of course not. I was professional."

She paused. "Define professional."

I flopped back in the chair, arms crossed. "I may have implied he was a mansplaining egomaniac with a God complex."

Mia blinked. "Wow. Subtle."

"Ugh. He's the worst."

"Uh-huh," she said, still sketching.

I squinted at her. "What?"

She gave me a look. The kind of look that usually came with a warning siren and a flashing red light.

"So. You're obsessed with him."

I scoffed. "I hate him."

"Same thing."

"It is not the same thing. *Obsessed* implies I think about him constantly. I just want to make sure he doesn't destroy the company I've spent five years building. He's exactly the kind of guy who never had to try. The kind who thinks the world bends to his will because it always has."

"Mmm-hmm." She flipped a page. "Totally normal amount of rage-rambling about someone you don't care about."

"I'm venting! The meeting just happened!"

Mia tilted her head. "Uh-huh."

I sat up straighter. "Anyway, he had the nerve to tell me he'd 'heard good things' about my work. Like he's been studying up on all of us."

Her eyes flicked again, now fully intrigued. "Wait. He knew who you were?"

"Said he read the quarterly reports. Claims my name came up in his 'research'." I did air quotes again. "Like he actually combed through our client retention data."

But a tiny voice in my head whispered... *what if he had?* And why did that make my stomach do a weird little flip?

Mia grinned like the Chesire Cat. "Sounds like somebody met her match."

"He's insufferable."

"You're one printer jam away from hate-kissing him in the copy room."

"I would rather kiss an actual printer."

"That would void the warranty," Mia said with a smirk.

"At least the printer is honest about its intentions. It doesn't pretend to be something it's not."

"Kinky," Mia said, wiggling her eyebrows.

I stared at her. "You're dead to me."

Chapter Three

BRETT

I DIDN'T SCHEDULE THE meeting out of spite.

It was strategy. Precision.

After the leadership debrief, I already knew who I wanted to start with.

Elizabeth Bentley.

She'd lingered in my head longer than I wanted to admit. That glare. The razor-sharp mouth. The way she said *Brett* like she'd invented sarcasm just for me.

I told myself it was because I needed to determine if she was an asset or a liability.

Not because I was curious.

Not because I'd wondered what it would take to crack that steel exterior and make her forget to hate me for five seconds.

It was business.

She walked into my office exactly on time. Not a minute early. Not a second late.

Composed. Controlled. But the tension in her shoulders gave her away—the kind of stiffness that said *I've practiced this calm, and I will not break character.*

"Ms. Bentley," I said.

She nodded coolly. "Mr. Wentworth."

I gestured to the chair. "Please."

She sat like it was a trap. Straight back, legs crossed, hands folded so tight they might fuse together. Immaculately professional. Except for the eyes.

Those were already daring me to try something.

I opened her file—not because I needed it, but because looking at paper was safer than looking at her. "Five years at Bright Spark. Started in entry-level marketing. Promoted to account exec in three years."

"Two," she corrected a little too quickly.

I glanced up. That flash of tension in her jaw—there it was again.

"Your client retention rate is ninety-two percent. Highest in the company."

Her posture loosened by half a degree. "I prioritize relationships."

"So do your clients, apparently." I flipped to the next page. "Parkwood Elementary's principal called you 'indispensable.' Said you're the only reason they renewed this year."

A flicker of pride slipped through. "They were working with a shoestring budget. I restructured their plan so they could still use our products without overspending."

"At the expense of your commission."

She didn't blink. "It was the right call. And it's brought in three new accounts. Worth it."

I leaned back. The file said high-performer. But this? This was fire. Passion, laced with something else. Conviction. Sharp-edged and unapologetic.

That kind of intensity was valuable. Also volatile. Especially when it was aimed directly at me.

I shut the file. "Tell me something I won't find in here."

Her eyebrow lifted. "Excuse me?"

"Something personal. Something that explains why you fight like hell for clients who can barely afford the shipping fees."

She paused. Clearly didn't like the question.

But she didn't dodge it either.

"I was a scholarship kid," she said. "My mom taught first grade and waitressed on weekends. I watched her stretch paychecks and still come up short."

Her voice didn't waver, but it was lower now. Realer. "These kits? These aren't just toys. Not to people like her. They're what kids remember. What keeps them curious."

I caught it then—how she leaned in slightly, just enough to forget the performance. Her voice softened. Her guard didn't drop, but it shifted. Like maybe she didn't really hate me. Just didn't trust me yet.

And then I did the thing I hadn't meant to do.

I flipped to the section of her file that didn't match the rest.

"Your résumé says Stanford," I said. "But your file doesn't list a degree. Is there a reason for the discrepancy?"

Her expression changed so fast it could've given me whiplash.

Her voice was ice. "I completed seven semesters. I didn't finish. Personal reasons."

I waited. Let the silence stretch.

She didn't elaborate.

I nodded slowly. "Didn't seem to impact your performance."

"No," she said, lifting her chin a fraction. "It didn't."

Her tone was sharp again, polished with practiced armor. Like she'd been asked that question too many times—and had learned exactly how to make people regret it.

Most people I'd met here were either terrified of me or overly eager to please.

She was neither.

She wasn't trying to win me over—she was trying to keep me out.

And that, somehow, made me want to know everything.

LIZ

I kept my expression neutral. Steady. Unbothered.

"Personal reasons," I said, letting the words hang between us.

He didn't push. Just gave a slow, measured nod.

And that was somehow worse.

The professional distance of his reaction felt like a trap—as if he were waiting for me to volunteer more information, to expose a vulnerability he could use later.

I'd spent five years proving myself, and I wasn't about to let Billy—Brett—Wentworth undo all that with one glance at my incomplete education.

"Your numbers speak for themselves," he said after a beat, closing the file.

I nodded once—tight, clipped. Then stood.

He stood too.

Because, of course he did. Polite. Proper. Predictable.

I hesitated for half a second.

Technically, he'd called this meeting.

But I was done.

"Thanks for your time," I said, and even to my own ears, it sounded like I was trying not to choke on it.

He nodded again, that unreadable face still giving me absolutely nothing.

I turned on my heel and walked out.

The door clicked shut behind me.

And just like that, the calm gave way.

Not a breakdown. Not tears. Just that hollow, sinking weight pressing on my chest—the kind that creeps in when you've worked so hard to outrun your past, and suddenly, it catches up.

I knew that feeling.

I knew it because of *him*.

The Bradley Situation.

Bradley was the golden boy at Stanford—charm, confidence, and trust-fund swagger in one perfectly tousled package. He wore entitlement like a custom suit and had a smile built to disarm.

And for a while, it worked.

He made me believe I belonged.

He made me believe someone like him could want someone like me.

He didn't, not really.

While I was pulling all-nighters and obsessing over every detail, he was copying my assignments word for word and submitting them as his own.

I didn't know.

Not until the university flagged the overlap and launched an investigation.

He denied everything. Said I was the one who copied him.

And they believed him.

Of course they did.

He was a legacy with a donor dad and a spotless record.

I was a scholarship kid—smart but expendable.

His father wrote a check and Bradley walked across the graduation stage in a designer suit.

And I?

I packed up my dorm room and disappeared—one class short of a degree.

I didn't tell anyone.

Not my mom. Not my friends.

I rewrote the ending.

Polished the résumé.

Smiled when I said I'd taken a job early.

And for a while, I convinced myself it didn't matter.

That it hadn't wrecked me.

But it had.

And that's why I don't trust charm, or confidence, or a pretty boy with a family name and a carefully curated backstory.

It's why I see someone like Brett Wentworth and I already know exactly who he is. Exactly *what* he is.

Because I've lived that story.

And I barely made it out the first time.

Chapter Four

BRETT

"Let me guess," Logan said, settling into the chair across from me like he owned it. "First day as CEO, and you've already terrified half the executive team."

I didn't look up from my bourbon. "Not quite half."

"Ah. So modest."

He lounged back, annoyingly relaxed in one of his ridiculous Hawaiian shirts. Logan Dawson was the human equivalent of charm on tap—CEO of his own boutique travel company, unreasonably well-liked, and irritatingly perceptive when it came to me.

"You're supposed to ease into power," he said, propping one ankle over his knee. "Shake some hands. Flash that smolder you pretend isn't smoldering. Toss out a few buzzwords—'agile,' 'growth hacking,' and 'vertical synergy.' You know. Foreplay."

"I'm not interested in foreplay," I muttered.

Logan raised a brow. "And now I'm concerned. What did she do to you?"

I froze.

He grinned. "Ah. There it is."

"I don't know what you are talking about."

"Bullshit. You've got that look on your face. All broody and wound-up. Like someone questioned your authority, and you didn't hate it as much as you should've."

I took a slow sip. "Her name is Elizabeth Bentley. Senior account exec. Sharp. Passionate."

"Oh God," Logan sighed, delighted. "You're intrigued. You *hate* being intrigued."

I didn't respond.

"She challenged you," Logan said, more seriously now. "That's rare. Most people walk on eggshells around you."

"She was defensive," I said. "Borderline insubordinate."

Logan gave a low whistle. "Now I really wish I'd been there."

I didn't respond. Just took another sip.

"Let me guess—she sized you up and handed your ego back with a smile."

Sometimes I really hated Logan.

***

I returned to the office after dinner because I had work to do—files to review, departments to assess, people to evaluate.

The building was mostly dark when I stepped off the elevator. Quiet. Still.

I wasn't expecting anyone else.

Which is why I stopped short at the light glowing at the end of the hall.

Liz's office.

Of course she hadn't left.

I walked toward her door, drawn by an inexplicable curiosity I didn't want to examine too closely. The door was partially open, and a sliver of warm light spilled into the hallway.

I paused at the threshold, about to knock—then froze.

She was bent over, reaching for something that had fallen next to her desk. Her pencil skirt had ridden up, hugging the curves of her ass and thighs as she stretched forward, one hand braced on her desk, the other extended toward the floor.

And yeah, I noticed her ass.

Curvy. Perfectly distracting. The kind of view that punched straight through logic and professionalism like a wrecking ball.

I dragged my gaze away.

Or tried to.

But my body didn't get the memo.

Something primal kicked in, sending blood rushing south with embarrassing speed. To my complete irritation, I was getting hard—right there in the goddamn hallway like some hormone-addled teenager.

I shifted, adjusting my stance. What the hell was wrong with me? This woman was argumentative, standoffish, clearly gunning for my head. I didn't even like her.

And yet... here I was, ready to worship the ground beneath her heels.

I cleared my throat loudly—partly to alert her, partly to regain control.

She jerked upright, spinning around with wide eyes that narrowed the second they landed on me.

"What are you doing?" she demanded, voice sharp with embarrassment—and something else. Something that made my pulse jump.

"I saw the light," I said, aiming for neutral. "Didn't think anyone else was burning the midnight oil."

Her cheeks flushed, but she didn't look away. "Some of us don't have the luxury of clocking out early."

That one stung more than I cared to admit.

"Is that what you think I do?" I asked, taking a step into her office. The air between us felt charged, static crackling with tension.

"Isn't it?" she challenged, crossing her arms. The movement pushed her breasts together slightly under her silk blouse, and I forced my eyes to stay locked on hers.

"No. Actually, I was having dinner with a friend before coming back to review department files."

Her arms stayed crossed, but her chin lifted, eyes blazing. No hesitation—just a challenge.

"Let me guess—you've already decided who stays and who goes. Just another rich guy playing king."

There it was. The crack.

The one she didn't mean to show.

I stepped closer before I could stop myself.

"I'm just trying to understand who belongs here."

She didn't flinch. Just lit up like a match.

"You don't know me," she snapped. "You don't know what I've done to get here. What I've given up. But you think you can sit in your glass office and decide if I'm worth keeping?"

"That's not what I—"

Before I could finish, she poked me.

Right in the chest.

Hard.

And I don't know what surprised me more—the fire in her eyes or the jolt that ran through me at her touch.

LIZ

I meant it to be a statement. A shove. A reminder that I wasn't afraid of him—or the ridiculous power he carried with that last name and pressed suit.

I didn't expect my finger to land on solid muscle.

Hard muscle.

Not polished-gym-bro muscle. Not soft-rich-guy-who-hires-a-trainer muscle.

No—this was the kind of solid that said he did the work. Earned it.

Shit.

His eyes caught mine, and there was heat there. Awareness. A flicker of surprise that matched mine—only he didn't bother hiding it.

"You expected me to be soft," he said, low and infuriatingly calm.

I jerked my hand back like I'd touched a live wire. "Don't flatter yourself. I didn't expect anything."

His mouth curved into that half-smile that made my stomach do something deeply inconvenient. "Liar."

"I'm not lying," I snapped, though the heat crawling up my neck said otherwise.

We were close now. Too close for oxygen. Too close for good decisions.

Close enough to smell his cologne—not overpowering, not trying too hard. Just... expensive. Clean. The kind of scent that whispered lean in closer and not in a creepy way.

Which was precisely what I was *not* going to do.

"You're infuriating," I muttered.

"The feeling's mutual," he murmured, voice rougher now.

And then—he stepped even closer.

I should've walked away.

I didn't.

"I've met a hundred women like you," he said, and the rasp in his voice betrayed him. "All thinking they've got me figured out."

"And I've met a dozen men like you," I fired back. "Born on third base, convinced they hit a triple."

His jaw flexed.

"You don't know anything about me."

"I know enough," I said—and the words hung there, hot and electric, full of fire and something else I didn't dare name.

My nipples tightened beneath my blouse, and a rush of heat pulsed between my legs—hot, aching, traitorous.

I should've hated this. I was supposed to hate this.

Instead, my body was lighting up like it hadn't gotten the memo.

"You want me to be the villain," he said, voice dropping to a near-growl. "Because that's easier."

I scoffed—wobbly. "And why wouldn't I? Guys like you make it so damn easy."

A muscle ticked in his jaw as he leaned in. Heat rolled off him like a warning.

"You want to know what I think?" he said, voice low and dangerous. "I think you're terrified I might *not* be the villain you need me to be."

His eyes dropped to my mouth, and something inside me short-circuited.

My breath caught. My skin flushed. Every inch of me suddenly aware of just how close he was.

Brett Wentworth was going to kiss me.

And the worst part?

Some unhinged, completely traitorous part of me wanted him to.

"Don't," I whispered, before that part of me got louder.

But it didn't come out strong. It came out like a dare.

He didn't move—just hovered there, close enough that I could feel the heat rolling off him. His voice dropped, low and dangerous.

"Don't what?"

"Don't kiss me," I said.

It was supposed to be a warning.

It sounded like a challenge.

That smirk again. Like he could see straight through me and was enjoying every second of it.

"Is that what you think I'm going to do?"

My cheeks flamed. "Isn't it?"

He leaned in—just a breath from my ear, voice low enough to melt reason.

"I don't kiss women who hate me."

A shiver shot down my spine, sharp and electric.

And then—he stepped back.

The air snapped between us like a pulled wire, leaving me breathless, buzzing, and completely unmoored.

"Have a good night, Ms. Bentley," he said, maddeningly even, already turning away like nothing had happened.

The sudden distance hit like whiplash. One second, he was all heat and temptation—close enough to undo me. The next? Gone.

Which was good.

Exactly what I wanted.

Exactly what I needed.

Right?

Then why did my body still ache like he'd taken something with him when he walked away?

Chapter Five

LIZ

I COULDN'T SLEEP THAT night. The ceiling of my bedroom had never been fascinating, but at 2:37 am, I'd memorized every crack and shadow. My mind replayed that moment in my office like a broken record—the heat in his eyes, the way his voice dropped, the intoxicating scent of his cologne. And the way he'd just... walked away. "Ugh!" I groaned, flipping onto my stomach and burying my face in my pillow. This was ridiculous. I didn't want Brett Wentworth to kiss me. I didn't want anything from him except professional distance and maybe, eventually, a glowing reference when I inevitably left for a company not run by an arrogant billionaire. So why couldn't I stop thinking about how his lips might have felt against mine? I reached for my phone, tempted to text Mia, but I knew exactly what she'd say. Something about "hate-kissing" and "sexual tension" that I absolutely did *not* need to hear right now.

I tossed my phone aside. This was insane. I sat up with a deep, weary sigh and ran my fingers through my tangled hair, feeling each knot and stray strand as if they were manifestations of my inner chaos. I chided myself; I was a grown, successful woman who had faced intimidating corporate execs, negotiated six-figure deals, and once told a department head that his marketing strategy was "embarrassingly outdated." I wasn't the type to melt over a maybe. But then again, I'd never stood that close to a man whose presence felt like a promise—and a threat—all in one.

"This is just chemistry," I muttered. "Annoying. Distracting. Temporary."

A blip. A glitch. The kind of thing easily resolved with a glass of wine, some denial, and a little help from the right toy.

Driven by a desperate need to regain control over my spiraling thoughts, I rolled over and yanked open the bedside drawer. Amidst a jumble of chargers, lip balms, and miscellaneous clutter, my fingers closed around the smooth, cool silicone of my trusted vibrator. It was a gift from Mia last Christmas—a playful, almost scandalous token wrapped in festive paper and accompanied by a card that cheekily read, "For when spreadsheets aren't enough excitement." I had laughed then, half-embarrassed and half-grateful, pushing it aside with a fleeting blush of amusement.

Now, holding it in my palm, it felt like a symbol of rationality—a simple, clinical outlet to channel my tangled arousal away from the mess that was Brett Wentworth. It was just a release. A reset. A way to clear the fog and get back to what really mattered.

The first touch made me gasp—I was already aching in a way that betrayed just how worked up I'd been.

"Damn him," I whispered, closing my eyes as I pressed the vibrator more firmly against my clit.

But closing my eyes was a mistake. Because suddenly, he was there—those dark eyes, that voice like honey and sin. I could feel the ghost of his breath at my ear, the imagined heat of his shoulders under my palms.

"This isn't about him," I reminded myself, but my body disagreed. The tension was building fast, embarrassingly fast, my hips rising to meet each pulse of the vibrator as I imagined what might have happened if I hadn't said "don't." If he had closed that final inch between us.

"Fuck," I gasped, my free hand clutching at the sheets as I came hard and sudden, waves of pleasure crashing through me with an intensity that left me trembling.

As the aftershocks faded, so did the temporary fog of satisfaction. I lay there, breathing hard, irritation bubbling up beneath the surface. Of all the fantasies to hijack my brain, it had to be him. Brett freaking Wentworth. The man I was determined to loathe. A distraction in a tailored suit whose presence was already too dangerous to ignore—professionally or otherwise.

"This never happened," I declared firmly to my quiet, empty room, as if convincing the silence could erase the memory. I cleaned it—because I'm not a complete degenerate—tossed it back in the drawer, and slammed it shut. Great. Now I could add *horny for the enemy* to my list of professional concerns.

***

I spent the entire morning rehearsing.

Every stat. Every rebuttal. Every slide.

Twenty-eight pages of indisputable proof that I was an asset Bright Spark couldn't afford to lose.

No heat. No tension. Just cool, corporate precision.

"You've got this," I muttered, collecting my laptop, notes, and client testimonials like armor. "He's just a man. A frustrating, smug, dangerously attractive—no. Just a man. Who signs your paychecks."

Each step toward Brett's office felt like a reset.

Click. I'm a professional.

Click. I am exceptional at my job.

Click. And any resemblance between last night's fantasy and my boss is purely coincidental.

His assistant glanced up as I approached. "He's expecting you, Ms. Bentley. Go on in."

Brett stood by the window when I walked in, sleeves rolled up, tie loosened, forearms casually ruining my focus.

Not helpful.

"Mr. Wentworth," I said crisply. "I've prepared a detailed overview of my portfolio and performance over the last three years."

I placed my laptop on the conference table, my movements precise and controlled. Ice queen, fully activated.

He turned, taking his time crossing the room. Then he leaned against the edge of his desk, arms crossed, watching me like he was waiting for me to blink.

"Thank you for being so thorough," he said, voice calm and infuriatingly deep. "But before we get to your presentation, there's something else we need to talk about."

I froze. "And what would that be?"

"We have a problem, Ms. Bentley."

My fingers tightened around my pen. "I wasn't aware of any issues with my performance."

He stepped forward, slow and deliberate. "This isn't about your performance."

Oh no.

"I don't know what you're talking about," I said—fast, unconvincing.

He kept coming. That subtle cologne hit my senses like a tranquilizer dart wrapped in lust.

"I think you do," he murmured. "There's something happening here. And it's getting harder to ignore."

"Mr. Wentworth—"

"Brett."

"I prefer Mr. Wentworth," I snapped, even as my voice wobbled. "And there is nothing between us."

His gaze swept over me. Calm. Too calm. "Then why can't you look me in the eye when you say that?"

I did. "I'm looking. And I'm telling you—we're strictly professional."

He stepped closer.

I backed up—straight into the conference table.

"Sure," he said, voice like velvet over steel. "That's why you're clutching that folder like it's a flotation device."

I glared. "You are wildly full of yourself."

"You were thinking about last night."

My breath caught.

Wait—what?

How the hell could he possibly know what I did last night?

He couldn't.

There's no way.

Unless he'd suddenly developed telepathy—or my vibrator had started sending status reports.

He tilted his head. "How I didn't kiss you."

Oh.

My stomach dropped—for a completely different reason.

Damn him.

"You're imagining things."

His lips curved. That maddening almost-smile. "Am I?"

He closed the distance, heat radiating off him like a furnace.

"Because I've been thinking about it too."

My pulse thundered in my throat.

"That's inappropriate, Mr. Wentworth."

"So is the way you're looking at me right now."

This was a nightmare.

A tall, broad-shouldered, unfairly attractive nightmare who smelled like bad choices and sin and made my brain short-circuit.

"I came here to discuss my job," I said tightly, gripping my folder like it might save me.

"And I came here to figure out why I can't stop thinking about you."

My mouth opened. Closed. Useless.

"Can we start the presentation?"

He smiled—slow, smug, and absolutely devastating.

"You're adorable when you're flustered."

"I'm not flustered."

"Keep telling yourself that."

His smile said he saw right through me.

And unfortunately, he wasn't wrong.

BRETT

She was flushed and breathless, her chest rising like she'd just run a mile. My presence was getting to her—and hell if that didn't light something dark and hungry in me.

"You want to hate me," I said, stepping close enough to feel her warmth. "It'd be a lot easier if you could."

"I do hate you," she snapped—too fast, too breathless.

That defiant gleam in her eyes? Still there. But now it was tangled with something else. Want. Sharp and raw and aimed straight at me.

"No," I murmured, inching closer. "You don't. And it's driving you crazy."

She didn't move. Didn't speak. She just stood there with her lips parted and her spine ramrod straight, as if her pride was the only thing holding her upright.

"Tell me to back off," I said low. "Tell me there's nothing here, and I'll step away. We'll go over your presentation like professionals. Like nothing happened."

She didn't.

Her eyes flicked to my mouth, and that was it. The last thread snapped.

I cupped her jaw gently, brushing my thumb along her cheekbone. "Last chance."

Her answer was a fistful of my shirt and a kiss that knocked the air from my lungs.

It was fire. It was the kind of kiss that stripped you bare—fast, fierce, and fucking inevitable.

She kissed like she fought—unyielding, intense, demanding. Our mouths clashed, tongues tangling, bodies colliding like we'd been circling this moment from the start.

I groaned into her mouth, dragging her closer. She gasped when I lifted her onto the table, and her legs wrapped around me instinctively. I pressed into her, letting her feel every hard inch of what she was doing to me.

"I hate you," she whispered against my lips, even as she arched into my touch.

"Sure you do," I growled, trailing my mouth along her neck.

My hands slid up her thighs, bunching her skirt. When I finally slipped my hand between her legs, I felt it—damp lace, hot aching need. And fuck if that didn't undo me.

"You're so fucking wet." I murmured, voice rough. "Tell me again how much you hate me."

She whimpered when I rubbed her through the fabric. Her fingers clenched my shoulders, nails digging in.

"I—loathe you," she panted, hips grinding down against my hand.

I chuckled against her throat. "That so?"

She tugged my hair—hard. "Don't stop."

That was all I needed.

I pushed her panties aside, sliding one finger into her slick heat. She clenched around me, tight and perfect. Her lips parted in a breathy moan that went straight to my cock.

"Fuck," I muttered. "You feel incredible."

"Brett." My name came out like a plea.

I added a second finger, my thumb circling her clit. Her body rocked against me, breath hitching, eyes fluttering shut.

"That's it," I whispered. "Come for me, Elizabeth. Show me how much you don't want this."

She trembled, head thrown back, muscles tightening. I watched it hit her—the way she shattered, silently at first, then with a gasp that would haunt my dreams. Her body pulsed around my fingers, her thighs trembling.

I kissed her hard as she came, swallowing the moan that ripped out of her. When she slumped against me, dazed and wrecked, I slowly pulled my fingers free, watching her reaction.

Her gaze was heavy-lidded. Lips kiss-swollen. Hair slipping from her ponytail.

I brought my fingers to my lips and sucked them clean—slow, deliberate, never breaking eye contact.

She stared, jaw slack.

"Jesus," she whispered.

"You taste even better than I imagined," I said softly.

A knock shattered the moment.

"Mr. Wentworth?" my assistant called through the door. "Your two o'clock is here early."

I froze.

Another knock.

"Just a moment," I called, fighting to steady my breathing.

Elizabeth was already moving, pulling her skirt down, smoothing her blouse, and brushing trembling fingers through her hair. She wouldn't look at me.

I tucked in my shirt and straightened my tie, though my body was still coiled with want.

"We're not done," I said, stepping toward her.

Her eyes flew to mine, wide and burning. "Yes, we are. This—" her voice cracked, "was a mistake."

I flinched.

"Elizabeth, wait. We'll talk after—"

"There's nothing to say," she bit out. "It meant nothing."

"Liz—"

"Don't call me that," she said, voice low and sharp. "You don't get to call me that."

And then she was gone.

The door clicked shut behind her, leaving behind the echo of her voice, the heat of her body, and the storm we'd just unleashed—raw, reckless, impossible to ignore.

Chapter Six

LIZ

I STORMED PAST BRETT'S assistant like a woman possessed, ignoring the poor guy in reception who blinked at me like I might explode. Honestly, he wasn't wrong to be scared.

I stabbed the elevator button like it owed me money. When the doors opened, I practically dove inside and collapsed against the wall, heart pounding. The second they slid shut, I let out a sound that was half-wheeze, half-deranged laugh.

Oh. My. God.

I had just— He had just— We had just—

"Shit. Shit. Shit."

My underwear was still damp. My pulse was still thudding. And the man responsible?

Brett freaking Wentworth.

The man I was supposed to hate.

The man who signs my paychecks.

The man who now knew *exactly* what I sounded like mid-orgasm.

Amazing. Love that for me.

Downstairs, the receptionist gave me a once-over that clearly said: *damn, girl*—like she couldn't decide whether to call security or offer me a glass of water.

I didn't stop. I shot out the building like daylight might somehow scorch the memory off my skin.

Spoiler: it didn't.

By the time I got home, I looked like I'd barely survived a rave. Ponytail half-collapsed, lipstick smudged, blouse askew—like I'd stumbled through a battlefield instead of a boardroom.

I slammed the door behind me and kicked off my heels with enough force to launch one under the couch. Good. Let it live there.

"What the hell were you thinking?" I hissed at my reflection.

The woman staring back at me? She didn't look like Elizabeth Bentley: competent, capable, senior account executive.

She looked like someone who'd just short-circuited her entire life for a man with great bone structure and hands that could ruin empires.

I yanked off my jacket like it had betrayed me and stomped into the bedroom, stripping as I went.

The blouse? Gone.

The skirt? Dead to me.

The lace underwear? Gone. Tossed into the hamper like it personally betrayed me.

I caught sight of myself again in the mirror. Flushed. Damp. Eyes blown wide with leftover lust.

"Pull it together," I muttered, stomping into the bathroom and cranking the shower like I wanted to steam-clean my brain.

The water scalded. Didn't help.

I scrubbed until my skin turned pink and my heart finally slowed. But the echo of his voice still hummed in my ear. The ghost of his mouth still tingled on mine. And between my thighs? A memory I couldn't shake.

Wrapped in the biggest towel I owned, I collapsed onto the edge of the bed.

My phone buzzed.

Of course it did.

Mia:

Where did you go???

*Diana from accounting said you **ran**.*

Are you okay???

Elizabeth Bentley, I swear to God, if you don't answer me, I'm coming over.

With wine.

And snacks.

And QUESTIONS.

I groaned and hit call. She picked up on the first ring.

"Oh THANK GOD, she *lives*," Mia said. "I was about to file a missing persons report and list your last known location as 'inside your own corporate shame spiral'."

"I'm fine," I lied. Badly.

"Try again."

"I got a migraine."

"Bullshit. You get stress headaches and power through them like a demon in heels."

"Mia—"

"Wait." A beat. "Did he fire you?"

I let out a too-loud, slightly manic laugh. "No. He... *definitely* didn't fire me."

"Elizabeth Marie Bentley," she said, voice deadly serious. "What happened?"

"Nothing."

"Oh. My. God. You hooked up with him."

"No."

"You *so* did! Was it a kissing moment? A desk moment? A public-indecency-and-an-HR-lawsuit moment?"

I flopped back onto the bed with a groan. "It was one moment. A heat-of-the-moment, hormones-hijacked-my-brain moment."

Mia gasped so loud I had to yank the phone away from my ear.

"You did the deed in his office, didn't you?"

"No one did any deed!"

"Then what *did* happen?"

"We kissed. There may have been fingers involved. It was... a very poor choice."

There was a pause. Then:

"Tell me everything. Right now. Or I swear I'll haunt your ass forever."

"I'm never going back to the office again."

"Yes, you are. And when you do, I want you looking like the patron saint of bad decisions—with a killer strut and absolutely no regrets."

I sighed. "I hate you."

"No you don't. But you *do* have it bad."

I hung up before she could say *hot and bothered* again.

Then I lay there, towel slipping, chest heaving, heart pounding.

What the hell had I done?

And worse—

Why did part of me want to do it again?

BRETT

I left the office after my two o'clock meeting.

Not because the day was done—far from it—but because I couldn't sit in that building one second longer without thinking about what had happened in my damn office.

I didn't say anything to my assistant on the way out. Just grabbed my jacket, shut the door behind me, and headed straight to the elevator like I had someplace important to be.

My car was waiting out front.

My driver raised an eyebrow when I slid into the backseat—it wasn't exactly quitting time—but he didn't comment. Just pulled away from the curb like we did this every day.

'Home, sir?' he asked after a beat

"Yeah," I said quietly. "Home."

I wasn't heading home to relax or clear my schedule. I just needed space—from the woman who'd short-circuited every logical thought I'd had since walking into Bright Spark.

I stared out the window, jaw tight, fists clenched in my lap.

I almost told him to take a detour. Just a quick stop. Just to check on her.

But I didn't.

Because I knew if I saw her again tonight, I wouldn't be able to keep my hands off her. Wouldn't be able to think straight. Wouldn't stop at just touching her. I would tear her fucking clothes off and bury myself so deeply in that hot tight pussy that I wouldn't know where I ended, and she began.

The car rolled to a stop in front of my building. I stepped out without a word, and the doorman greeted me as I crossed the marble lobby.

"Good evening, Mr. Wentworth."

I managed a curt nod in response, already jabbing the elevator button. The doors slid open immediately as if sensing my urgency. My reflection stared back from the mirrored walls—flushed face, disheveled hair, eyes dark with barely contained need.

I looked like a man on the edge.

The elevator ascended to the penthouse, and I was grateful for the privacy. My cock had been painfully hard since the moment her lips touched mine, and the pressure of my slacks was becoming unbearable. Her taste was still on my tongue, her scent on my fingers, and I could hear the little gasp she'd made when I'd slid my fingers inside her.

"Fuck," I growled, tossing my keys onto the marble counter with enough force to send them skidding across the surface.

I needed a drink. A cold shower. A lobotomy. Anything to get Elizabeth Bentley out of my head.

I poured three fingers of whiskey, not bothering with ice, and downed half of it in one burning swallow. The alcohol hit my system but did nothing to cool the heat raging through me. If anything, it just loosened what little restraint I had left.

I stalked to the floor-to-ceiling windows that overlooked the city. The sun was setting, painting it in shades of gold and amber. Somewhere out there, Elizabeth was probably cursing my name, trying to convince herself that what happened was a mistake.

But it wasn't. It was fucking inevitable. She just hadn't accepted it yet.

I drained the rest of my whiskey, feeling it burn all the way down. Setting the glass on the side table with more force than necessary, I unbuttoned my shirt, suddenly feeling confined. Constrained. Like my own fucking skin was too tight.

The memory of her taste lingered on my tongue—sweet, tangy, addictive. I wanted more. A lot more. And that terrified me.

I wasn't used to wanting something I couldn't have. Wasn't used to this gnawing, insistent ache that wouldn't subside no matter how much I tried to ignore it.

I stripped off my shirt and headed for the shower, turning the water as cold as possible. The icy spray hit my overheated skin like needles, but it did nothing to cool the fire burning inside me. If anything, the sensation just heightened everything—every nerve ending, every memory of her body against mine.

"Goddammit," I muttered, bracing one hand against the tile wall.

I gave in to the inevitable, wrapping my hand around my aching cock. The first stroke sent a jolt of pleasure so intense it bordered on pain. I closed my eyes, and she was there—those blue eyes challenging me, that mouth parted in a silent gasp, those fingers digging into my shoulders as she came undone.

I stroked harder, faster, imagining what it would have been like if we hadn't been interrupted. If I'd spread her thighs and buried myself deep inside her. The sounds she would have made. The way she would have felt, hot and tight around my cock.

"Elizabeth," I groaned, the sound echoing off the shower walls as I came hard, spilling over my hand. The release was intense but hollow—a poor substitute for what I really wanted.

I stayed under the cold spray for several minutes, trying to regain some semblance of control. But I knew it was pointless. Something fundamental had shifted today, and there was no going back.

Chapter Seven

BRETT

WHEN MIA CORNERED ME in the elevator the next morning and said, "You're coming to the prototype floor," I thought she was joking.

She wasn't.

"Investor tour's tomorrow," she added, already texting someone—possibly Satan. "You can't pitch what you haven't experienced. Liz is setting up the Adventure Kit now."

Of course she was.

Because nothing screams *let's pretend our wildly inappropriate office hookup never happened* like foam swords and suction-cup arrows.

I stepped into the prototype room, and there she was.

Liz.

Bent over a crate of gear, blonde curls pulled back, blouse tucked into a pencil skirt that should not have been legal this early in the morning.

She looked up.

Our eyes locked for one loaded, breathless second.

Then she blinked—armor slamming into place.

Chin up. Mouth tight. Sarcasm cocked and ready.

"Let me guess," she said, tone cool enough to chill concrete. "Mia threatened you."

"She's terrifying," Liz muttered, yanking a foam sword from a crate like she wanted to stab something. Possibly me. "But she's not wrong. Investors eat this stuff up."

The air between us was charged—every breath thick with the memory of last night. Her legs wrapped around me. Her moan in my ear. The way she'd whispered my name like a secret.

I cleared my throat. "So. Where do you want me?"

She hesitated.

Not long. Not noticeably. But enough.

Enough to know I wasn't the only one remembering.

Then, without looking at me, she nodded toward the far end of the setup. "Start at the tunnel. Try not to sprain anything."

There it was—dismissive, efficient, and just sharp enough to cut.

I deserved it.

But fuck if it didn't make me want her all over again.

I looked around the obstacle course like it was a war zone. Foam tunnels. Rope coils. A warning sign that read *LAVA PIT: DO NOT CROSS.*

"This is for the demo?"

"Yep." Liz knelt beside a bin of suction darts, her ponytail swaying as she pulled out gear. "Build-Your-Own Quest Kit. Ages six to ten. Obstacle pieces, costumes, a mission scroll, and enough ways to humiliate yourself to last a lifetime." She stood and tossed me a rope coil like it was a grenade. "You'll fit right in."

"I don't play," I said flatly.

She smiled sweetly. "You're about to. Use your imagination. Builds character."

Ten minutes later, I was tangled in netting, wedged halfway through a foam tunnel that was definitely not built for a six-foot-four adult male.

Leaning casually against the wall, Liz crossed her arms, biting back a grin.

"You look comfy," she said.

"This is a trap."

"You're just mad a ten-year-old would've beat your time."

"I'm six-foot-four."

"All that height and no coordination. It's tragic, really."

I finally crawled out, pride limping behind me. Foam bits clung to my pants. My shirt was untucked. My dignity was on life support.

"You're enjoying this," I muttered.

Liz didn't even try to deny it. "Watching you get outsmarted by a children's obstacle course? Highlight of my week."

Her eyes sparkled—real this time, unguarded. And when our eyes met, the moment stretched. A flicker of something passed between us, something warm and dangerous, like we were both remembering and pretending not to.

Then she turned, already reaching for the next setup.

"Come on, Wentworth," she called over her shoulder. "Let's see if you can survive the suction dart gauntlet."

"How'd you come up with this?" I asked.

She blinked, instantly more guarded. "What?"

"This kit. Mia said it was yours."

Her posture tightened for a beat—then she lifted her chin. "We brainstormed the idea together. But the layout? The mechanics? That's me."

I nodded. "It's smart. Really smart. And fun. Engaging. It's kind of... brilliant."

Her lips parted like she wanted to argue. Then shut again.

"It makes sense now," I said. "Why you fight so hard for this place."

She hesitated, the shield not quite back up. "It matters. To a lot of people."

I nodded. "Yeah. I'm starting to get that."

Then she tilted her head. "What about you?"

"What about me?"

"Why are you really here?" she asked. Not accusing. Just... curious.

"You could've walked away," she said. "Sold the company. Let someone else clean up the mess. But you didn't."

I looked at her. Really looked at her. And gave her the truth.

"I was running my own company," I said. "Logistics—warehousing, supply chain, the boring stuff that keeps the world spinning. I built it from nothing. Scaled it. Sold it for a number that still feels fake."

She didn't blink.

"I didn't use my dad's name. Didn't take a cent from him. I was tired of people thinking I was just coasting on someone else's legacy."

A flicker of something crossed her face. Her spine stayed straight, her jaw firm—but her cheeks flushed, just slightly.

She had the grace not to look away.

I paused. Then: "And then my dad called."

Her posture shifted. Just slightly.

"He told me Bright Spark was drowning. Contracts tanking. Clients bailing. Half the staff gone. And he hadn't even noticed—until it was almost too late."

I looked down at the foam sword in my hands.

"I could've let it fall. But I couldn't stop thinking about what it was supposed to be."

I turned the sword slowly in my fingers.

"When I was a kid, all I wanted was for my dad to pay attention, to play with me. Not big things. Just time. Focus. Not a tablet and a distracted 'go play.' But something real."

I looked at her again.

"That's what Bright Spark was supposed to be. A way for kids to imagine. Connect. Be seen. I didn't have that. But I could help make sure other kids did."

"You're not what I expected," she said softly.

I met her gaze. "Neither are you."

LIZ

I wasn't ready for that.

Not the story.

Not the quiet way he told it.

Not the gut-punch realization that I'd had him all wrong.

I'd painted Brett Wentworth in bold, unapologetic strokes: entitled, arrogant, probably had a yacht named after his golden retriever.

But this?

He hadn't coasted. He'd clawed his way to success, built something real, and stayed when he could've walked away from his father's mess.

And dammit, that did something to me.

Something warm and terrifying and way too inconvenient.

I looked away, mostly so he couldn't see the expression flickering across my face—whatever it was. But he didn't press.

He just stood there. Still. Steady. Present.

Which somehow made it worse.

"I used to think," I said before I could stop myself, "that if I just worked hard enough, no one could take anything from me."

He turned slightly toward me. Listening.

"I was the girl with the color-coded planner. Honor student. Every scholarship form submitted six weeks early." I let out a laugh that felt hollow. "None of it mattered."

I paused. Took a breath. The kind that felt like bracing for impact.

"There was this guy in college. Bradley." I didn't bother hiding the bitterness in my voice. "I thought he cared about me. I thought we were something real. But I was wrong. He used me. Copied my work—word for word. He got caught... and blamed me."

I swallowed.

"He had a last name that opened doors. A dad with deep pockets. I had a partial scholarship and an academic advisor who barely remembered my name."

I looked down at my hands. "He graduated. I didn't. One class short."

The silence stretched again.

"I never told anyone," I added, voice quieter now. "Not even my mom. I just... rewrote the story."

And now, it was out there.

Raw.

True.

I glanced at Brett.

No pity. No judgment.

Just... understanding.

And somehow, that was worse than pity.

Because suddenly, I didn't feel like I was staring at the enemy.

I felt like I was standing across from someone who knew exactly what it meant to be underestimated.

He leaned in, just enough to make my breath hitch.

His hand lifted—hesitating in the space between us.

Like he didn't know if he should touch me.

And God help me, I wanted him to.

But before he could—

"Hey!" Mia's voice rang from the hallway. "How's it going in—oh."

She stepped inside, blinked once, then smiled like she knew a secret we didn't.

"Well. No one's bleeding. That's a win."

I jerked back like we'd been caught making out behind the gym. "We were just wrapping up."

Mia glanced between us, eyes dancing. All sunshine and chaos. "Uh-huh. Well, I need you to look at the new prototypes before I throw my laptop, and myself, out the nearest window. You good here, Brett?"

He nodded once. Cool. Controlled. Already rebuilding whatever wall I'd watched crack just moments ago.

I nodded too—too fast. "Right. Yes. Prototypes. Absolutely."

Mia arched an eyebrow but didn't say anything. Just bumped me with her elbow, like she hadn't just interrupted a moment with a capital *M*, and turned for the hallway.

I followed, pulse still skittering.

And I didn't look back.

Because I wasn't entirely sure I'd be able to walk away if I did.

Chapter Eight

BRETT

Investor tours were always a performance.

Polished smiles. Polite nods. Just enough innovation to dazzle, just enough stability to soothe.

But today?

Today felt different.

Maybe because the stakes were higher.

Maybe because the company's future was riding on this.

Or maybe because every time I looked across the room and saw Liz—confident, poised, utterly magnetic—something inside me shifted.

She led a group of investors through the Adventure Kit demo, explaining how the obstacle components promoted movement, problem-solving, and teamwork. Her voice was clear and warm.

"She's good," Mia said beside me, not even pretending to be casual.

"I know," I said.

And I did. God, I did.

She was everything this company was supposed to be—clever, innovative, fearless. Watching her command the room felt like watching the future unfold in real time.

I barely had time to let that thought settle when the elevator dinged.

And everything inside me went still.

William Wentworth II.

Custom suit. Power tie. That arrogant glint in his eye like he'd just walked into *his* empire.

"What the hell is he doing here?" Mia muttered.

"No clue," I said, already bracing.

The air shifted the second he stepped out. Conversations stalled. Postures straightened. Most of the investors recognized him instantly.

My father smiled like a man who still thought the room belonged to him.

"Good morning! What an incredible showing. Wonderful to see such excitement about Bright Spark's future."

Liz paused mid-sentence. Turned.

Found me across the room.

Her eyes narrowed—confused. Guarded. A silent, *What is happening?*

I started toward her. One step. Two.

And then my father kept talking.

"I just want to say how proud I am of the leadership here," he said, voice booming. "Especially my son, Brett."

No.

"This," he gestured to the setup, "is exactly the kind of creativity I envisioned when I stepped aside."

No. No. **NO**.

"I was blown away," he went on, "when Brett brought me the Adventure Kit. He said, 'Let's give kids a way to imagine again. Let's get them moving.' And I thought—this, *this* is leadership!"

Polite applause followed. Tepid. Obligatory.

But I didn't hear any of it.

Because the moment William started talking, Liz had gone quiet.

Mid-sentence, mid-presentation—just... stopped.

Now she stood frozen across the room, still and silent.

Her gaze cut to my father.

Then to me.

And I saw the exact second her expression changed.

Not to anger. Not even to hurt.

To something worse.

Resignation.

The kind that said, *of course.* Like she'd been foolish to believe it could ever end any other way.

She walked away and didn't look back—and somehow, that hurt more than if she'd told me off.

Mia who had been filming the investor preview, appeared at my elbow.

Her voice was low, cold. "Fix it."

So I did the only thing I could.

I stepped forward.

"Thank you, William," I said into the quiet. My voice was sharp. Flat. Hard.

The room turned to me. My father stilled.

"But, there's been a mistake."

A few eyebrows lifted.

"The Adventure Kit wasn't my idea. I didn't pitch it. I didn't design it. I didn't bring it to life."

A wave of confused murmurs rippled through the group.

"It was Elizabeth Bentley."

My father's jaw tightened.

"She and Mia Wilder co-developed the concept," I said. "Liz designed the structure, the framework, the mission system. Every interactive element you saw today? That was her."

Silence.

Wide eyes.

A few startled blinks.

"And I'm not going to take credit for her brilliance."

My father opened his mouth—probably to spin it—but I didn't let him.

"If you're impressed by today," I told the investors, "then you're impressed with her."

I turned on my heel and headed for the door.

I didn't know where she'd gone.

But I wasn't letting her walk away. Not like this.

LIZ

The elevator doors slid shut behind me, but William Wentworth's voice still echoed in my ears.

Brett's idea.

Brett's pitch.

Brett's execution.

I didn't wait. Just walked—out of the elevator, down the hall, through the lobby—past the receptionist without so much as a glance.

Under the Bright Spark logo I used to be proud to walk beneath.

My vision blurred, but I didn't cry. Not here.

I just kept moving. Out into the spring air that felt too bright, too sharp—like the world hadn't gotten the memo that everything had just cracked apart.

Half a block later, I dropped onto a bench facing the park. Breathing like it required effort. Like my body had to manually remind itself how.

And then it hit me. Nausea, swift and brutal. Not just from the adrenaline crash, but from the truth settling in my gut.

He let it happen.

Brett.

He stood there and let his father rewrite my work into *his* legacy.

The same man who told me I mattered.

Who crawled through foam tunnels just to make me laugh.

Who opened up about his childhood and wanting something real.

And because he let me in—I let him in, too.

I told him about Bradley. About the sleepless nights and the stolen future.

Because his family had legacy status and lawyers on speed dial—and mine had work-study and scholarships.

I told Brett everything.

And I really thought—maybe this time would be different.

But it wasn't.

He stayed silent.

And something in me broke.

The hope I'd been holding onto cracked apart in that quiet.

I don't know how long I sat there.

Just long enough for the adrenaline to drain, for the humiliation to settle in, and for the awful truth to sink deep—

I let him matter.

And now I wished I hadn't.

Then—

"Liz."

I didn't turn.

He approached slowly, like I might spook and bolt.

Smart of him.

"Please," he said softly. "Let me explain."

I laughed.

Brittle. Cold. The kind of laugh that kept heartbreak from slipping through.

"Sure. Go ahead. Spin your version. Make it sound noble."

He flinched.

Good.

"Liz, I didn't know he was going to say that." His voice was rough. Unsteady. "I didn't even know he was going to be there. I never told him the Adventure Kit was my idea. I haven't even spoken to him in weeks. You have to believe me."

I turned to face him, every nerve ending flaring like a warning light. "You stood there while he handed you credit for something *I* built. And you said *nothing*."

"I did," he said quickly. "After you walked out—"

"Too late." My voice wavered, but I held the line.

He looked gutted.

And maybe he had tried.

But the damage was done.

"I told you about Bradley." The words came out soft—barely more than a breath. "I told you what it felt like to be erased. And you let it happen again."

His jaw tensed. "It wasn't the same—"

"It was exactly the same."

That landed.

Sharp and clean and cruel.

"You knew what that moment meant," I said. "You knew. And you still stood there."

I stepped past him.

No hesitation.

No glance back.

Because for the first time since he walked into my life, I saw him for who he really was.

And I wasn't about to let *Billy* Wentworth be the one who broke me.

Chapter Nine

BRETT

I DIDN'T GO AFTER her.

By the time I got my feet to move, she was already down the block.

She didn't look back.

She didn't have to.

I'd already seen it on her face—not anger, but something heavier.

Disappointment.

Like she'd expected better... and realized too late that I wasn't it.

And honestly? I couldn't blame her.

She'd trusted me—with the kind of truth you don't hand out unless you think someone's different. Safer. Worth the risk.

· And then my father stood there and took credit for her work, and I stayed silent.

Not forever.

Just long enough to feel like betrayal.

She told me what it cost her last time. What it felt like to be erased. And I let her think I'd done the same thing.

I pulled out my phone. Stared at it.

Then hit call.

Logan picked up on the first ring.

"Please tell me you're free to get a drink."

"Define *free*," he said.

There was a pause. A shuffle. Then, a shift in tone:

"Yes, ma'am, one mojito coming right up."

I blinked. "What the fuck—?"

"Hang on, sunshine, gotta fetch more limes."

"Logan." I said it like a threat.

"I'm at one of the resorts," he said, way too casually. "Site visit. Got mistaken for staff."

I snorted. "That's what you get for wearing those stupid Hawaiian shirts and flip-flops instead of dressing like a respectable CEO."

"I am *deeply* respected," he said. "Especially by the red-head who now thinks I coordinate guest experiences and lead sunset hikes."

"You're a menace."

"I'm thriving."

I exhaled hard, dragging a hand down my face. "I'm losing my damn mind."

"Okay. No jokes for a second—what happened?"

I didn't say anything—but apparently, I didn't need to. Logan's tone softened.

"This about her?"

"She walked out. Didn't look back."

"...Shit."

"Yeah."

"You want me to come back?"

"No. You've got beach chairs to alphabetize."

"She also thinks I lead paddleboard yoga at sunrise. Naturally, I've committed."

"You should be committed. Preferably somewhere with padded walls and no Wi-Fi. I hope she writes a scathing review."

"She's writing a *feature*," Logan said proudly. "And if it doesn't include the phrase *'charmingly rogue guest coordinator'*, I'll be devastated."

I groaned. "You're the reason warning labels exist."

"And you're spiraling," he said. "Go fix it."

LIZ

The spoon scraped the bottom of the pint with a sad little rustle—like even the ice cream was judging me.

I stared down at the empty container in my lap.

Contemplated the freezer.

Pint number two—chocolate fudge brownie—was in there. Tempting me with the kind of sweet nothings that always end in regret.

I didn't move.

Instead, I sighed and sank deeper into the couch cushions like a human burrito of regret.

My phone buzzed.

Again.

Another text from Mia. Number eight, if you were counting. (I was.)

Buzz. Nine.

Buzz. Ten.

I groaned. "Mia, if this is another cat meme, I swear—"

I flipped the phone over.

MIA:

You're going to regret ignoring me.

You need to watch this.

Seriously, Liz. Just watch it.

A video file waited beneath her text.

My thumb hovered.

Then tapped.

The screen lit up: the investor floor. The place where everything went to hell.

My stomach clenched, but I kept watching.

William Wentworth was mid-speech, soaking up credit he hadn't earned.

My fists clenched.

But then—

"There's been a mistake," Brett said.

My head snapped up.

"The Adventure Kit wasn't my idea I didn't pitch it. I didn't design it. I didn't bring it to life. That was Elizabeth Bentley."

Wait—what?

The camera was angled toward the front, but behind Brett, I caught it.

A flash of movement.

Me.

Still in the room.

He'd started speaking—*before* I walked out.

I just hadn't heard him.

Because I hadn't let myself.

I'd been so caught in the past—betrayal, heartbreak, and *Bradley*—that I never even gave Brett a chance to be anything else.

But he told the truth.

Right there. In front of investors. In front of his father.

"If you're impressed today, then you're impressed with her."

He looked wrecked in the video. Not smug. Not polished.

And I had walked out.

Not because he failed me.

Because I didn't wait long enough to see him *not* fail.

I set the phone down, heart pounding, throat tight.

God, I'd been so sure. I was so absolutely certain I knew what had happened. And I was wrong.

Brett hadn't taken anything.

He'd tried to fix it.

He'd defended me when it mattered.

And I'd missed it.

I swiped at my eyes. Stood up.

There was only one place I needed to be.

One man I needed to see.

I just hoped I wasn't already too late.

***

I'd never been to Brett's building before.

I'd seen it, sure—sleek, quiet-rich, high-rise energy. Black stone. Gold trim. The doorman with a Bluetooth earpiece that probably ran diagnostics on satellites.

Inside, it looked like a museum, and a Scandinavian furniture store had a baby and raised it on prestige TV.

My flip flops squeaked on the marble as I crossed the lobby. The doorman looked up—sixties, polished, with the kind of raised eyebrow that could shatter your self-esteem.

"Can I help you, miss?"

"Hi. Yes. I'm here to see Brett Wentworth."

I sounded calm. Composed.

Like I hadn't just cried into a hoodie and demolished a pint of salted caramel ice cream with a soup spoon.

He scanned me—frizzy hair, smudged sweatshirt, tote bag half-falling off my shoulder.

His expression didn't shift, but the *judgment* radiated off him like fine cologne.

"I'm afraid Mr. Wentworth has no appointments listed this evening."

"I know. I mean—I don't have an appointment, but he knows me. Liz Bentley. We work together." My voice lifted slightly at the end, hopeful.

He blinked once. The kind of blink that said *Oh, honey. No.*

"Yes," I said firmly. "He does know me. Really."

A pause.

Then he gave a polite, practiced smile that somehow managed to say *You poor, delusional thing.*

"I'm afraid I can't let anyone up without prior authorization."

"Can't you just... call him?"

"I'm afraid I'm not at liberty—"

"Please." My voice cracked. "It's important."

He hesitated. Then reached for the phone.

"Name?"

"Liz Bentley." I repeated.

He nodded. Pressed a button. "Sir, I have a Ms. Bentley here asking to see you... Yes... Understood."

He hung up. Straightened his jacket.

"Mr. Wentworth said to send you up."

I exhaled.

"Elevator's on your right. Top floor." Then, with a faint smile, "And miss?"

I turned.

"You might want to fix your hair. Just a bit."

I blinked. "Right. Thanks."

I stepped into the elevator, nerves on fire.

And prayed I wasn't too late.

Chapter Ten

BRETT

I HAD JUST POURED myself a drink I didn't need—bourbon, with a splash of guilt—when the phone buzzed.

"Sir, I have a Ms. Bentley here asking to see you."

I froze.

Liz. Here.

After everything.

"Send her up," I said before I could overthink it.

I didn't know what she was going to say. Hell, I didn't even know what *I* was going to say. But I knew one thing for sure:

I wasn't letting her walk away again.

The private elevator chimed.

I turned.

And there she was.

Hair a little windblown, hoodie zipped halfway up, tote bag sliding off her shoulder like it was clinging to her out of pure desperation. She looked unsure.

And completely beautiful.

Then she drew in a breath and stepped out.

"I saw the video," she said, voice quiet but steady.

My pulse kicked up. "What video?"

"Mia filmed the investor pitch." A humorless laugh escaped her. "Caught the whole thing—including you. Telling the truth. Giving me credit."

I blinked. "You watched it?"

She nodded. "Saw myself walk out right as you started talking. I didn't hear a word of it. I was so sure..." She trailed off, the disbelief still there. "I thought I knew exactly what happened."

I stepped closer, slow and careful. "You were hurting. I get it."

She gave me a look. "I said some pretty awful things."

I shrugged. "Please. You've called me worse—this week."

Her lips twitched, and for a second, I let myself hope.

We just stood there. No walls. No armor. Just everything unsaid hanging between us.

Then, she took another step forward.

"I was wrong," she said. "I should've stayed. I should've trusted you."

I shook my head. "You had every reason not to."

"Brett—"

"No, let me finish," I said gently. "What my father pulled today... I get why it hit the way it did. Some wounds don't heal all the way."

She nodded once.

"I had you pegged from day one," she said. "Trust fund guy. Polished. Entitled. I judged you before I even knew you."

"And now?"

"Now..." She met my eyes, honest and wide open. "I don't know. That's why I'm here."

My heart thudded. I closed the distance between us.

"Ask me," I said. "Anything."

She looked at me for a long beat. "Why did you really come to Bright Spark?"

"I told you before—it wasn't about saving my father's legacy. It was about the company. What it stood for." I paused. "But now? Now there's more."

"More?" she echoed, voice barely above a whisper.

"You." I stepped in closer.

"I've spent my whole life trying to prove I'm more than just a name. Then you walked into my office—sharp, stubborn—and saw exactly what everyone else sees."

She winced. "I did."

"I don't blame you. You weren't entirely wrong. I was born into privilege. A name. A legacy. But I built something of my own—no shortcuts, no handouts. And when my dad called about Bright Spark, I almost stayed away."

I paused.

"But I didn't. I showed up. And then I met you."

Her eyes softened.

"And suddenly, none of it was about legacy or redemption. It was about showing up for the things that matter. The ideas that matter. The people who matter. For you."

A long beat passed.

"You stood up for me," she said.

"I should've done it sooner."

"You did it when it mattered. When everyone who needed to hear it was listening."

"But you didn't hear it," I said quietly. "That's what kills me."

"I'm hearing it now," she whispered.

She stepped closer. So close I could feel the heat between us.

Then she reached up and touched my jaw—fingertips light like she wasn't sure I was real.

"I came here tonight because I needed to know," she said. "If what I saw in that video... was real."

I covered her hand with mine, pressing it to my cheek. "I'm real, Liz. What I feel for you is real."

Her eyes locked on mine. "And what do you feel?"

"Like you walked in, turned everything upside down, and somehow made it make more sense.

Her lips parted. Her breath caught.

"You walked in that first day like you were ready to set the building on fire," I said. "You've been under my skin ever since. You're brilliant. Relentless. Honest to a fault. And yeah, you make me crazy. But I want you. All of you. Not just the fire. I want the heart. The trust. The future."

She stared at me, eyes wide. "I don't do halfway, Brett."

"I'm not asking for halfway." I stepped even closer, our bodies nearly touching now. "I'm asking for everything."

The silence stretched. Not heavy. Not scary. Just full.

Then she smiled—small but sure.

"I want everything, too," she said.

And just like that—every breath I'd been holding released in one dizzying rush.

I cupped her face, brushing my thumb over her cheek. She leaned into the touch like she'd been waiting for it forever.

And maybe she had.

Because I knew I had.

"You sure?" I whispered.

"Ask me again after you kiss me," she whispered, a wicked little spark in her eyes.

LIZ

I breathed in, feeling my heart hammering against my ribs as Brett's eyes lingered on mine. The air between us crackled with electricity, with every confession and admission still hovering in the space we shared. He leaned in slowly, his hand sliding to the back of my neck, fingers tangling in my hair.

"Liz," he whispered, my name a prayer on his lips.

And then his mouth was on mine.

Not like before—frantic and desperate in his office. This was different. Deeper. Slower. Like he was memorizing me. His lips moved against mine with a tenderness that made my knees weak, a stark contrast to the heat building between us.

I melted into him, my hands sliding up his chest to grip his shoulders. He tasted like bourbon and promise—warm, rich, intoxicating. My tote bag slid from my shoulder, landing on the floor with a soft thud, but neither of us cared. Nothing mattered except this moment, this connection that felt like coming home after being lost for too long.

His arms wrapped around my waist, pulling me closer until there wasn't a breath of space between us. I gasped against his mouth as his tongue swept across my lower lip, seeking entrance. I opened to him without hesitation, my body arching into his as the kiss deepened.

When we finally broke apart, both breathing hard, his forehead rested against mine. His eyes were darker now, pupils blown wide with desire, but there was something else there too—vulnerability, honesty, raw emotion that made my chest ache.

"I've been thinking about you," he murmured, his voice rough and low. "Every day. Every night. Since that moment in my office."

My pulse quickened. "Have you?"

"Every minute," he confessed, his voice dropping to that delicious low register that made warmth pool in my belly. "I can't get you out of my head, Liz. The way you felt under my hands, the sounds you made, the taste of you—it's been driving me crazy."

The raw honesty in his admission sent a shiver down my spine. His hands slid to my waist, thumbs brushing against the sliver of skin where my hoodie had ridden up. Even that simple touch felt electric.

"I've been lying awake at night," he continued, "thinking about what would have happened if we hadn't been interrupted. Imagining all the ways I want to touch you, taste you."

I swallowed hard, my body responding to his words as intensely as his touch. The heat between us was building, transforming into something urgent and primal.

"Show me," I whispered, surprising myself with my boldness.

His eyebrows lifted slightly. "Show you what?"

I stepped back just enough to look at him fully, my heart pounding wildly against my ribs. The words formed on my lips before I could second-guess them.

"Show me what you do when you think about me," I said, my voice steadier than I felt. "When you're alone. I want to see what I've been missing."

His eyes darkened instantly, pupils dilating as his gaze swept over me. The intensity in his expression made my breath catch in my throat.

"Are you sure?" he asked, his voice a low rumble that I felt in my core.

I nodded, not trusting my voice. The anticipation building between us was almost unbearable.

Without breaking eye contact, Brett took my hand and led me deeper into his apartment, past the sleek living room with its floor-to-ceiling windows showcasing the glittering cityscape, toward what could only be his bedroom.

The space was minimalist but luxurious—a massive bed with charcoal sheets, ambient lighting that cast everything in a warm glow, and more of those incredible windows that made me feel like we were suspended in the night sky.

He turned to face me, his expression a mixture of desire and vulnerability.

Brett's eyes never left mine as he guided me to the edge of the bed. I sat down, my heart pounding so hard I was certain he could hear it. The city lights twinkled through the windows, casting his face in a play of shadow and light that made him look even more devastating.

"You're sure about this?" he asked again, his voice husky.

I nodded, finding my voice. "Yes. I want to see what I do to you. How you think of me when I'm not here."

Brett's jaw tightened, and for a moment I thought he might refuse. Then he nodded slowly, the intensity in his gaze making my skin tingle.

He inhaled sharply, his chest rising and falling with the effort. I could see the way his fingers flexed at his sides, like he was fighting to maintain control.

"I've never done this before," he admitted. "Not with someone watching."

The confession made my heart flutter. There was something incredibly powerful about being the first to see him this way—vulnerable, exposed, completely honest.

"I've never asked anyone before," I countered softly. "But I want to see you. All of you."

Brett held my gaze for a long moment, then nodded slowly. He stepped back, creating a small distance between us. With deliberate movements, he began to unbutton his shirt, one button at a time. I watched, transfixed, as each movement revealed more of his tanned skin, the trail of dark hair that disappeared beneath his waistband.

When his shirt finally slid from his shoulders, I couldn't help the small gasp that escaped me. Brett was gorgeous—broad shoulders, defined chest, abs that looked like they'd been sculpted from marble. But it wasn't just his physical perfection that made my mouth go dry; it was the raw vulnerability in his eyes as he stood before me, allowing me to see him.

"This is what you do to me," he said, voice rough as he unbuckled his belt. "Just thinking about you gets me hard."

The sound of his zipper sliding down made my pulse jump. He pushed his pants down his legs, stepping out of them with a grace that shouldn't have been possible in such an intimate moment. Standing before me in just his boxer briefs, the hard outline of his arousal was unmistakable.

I swallowed hard, my fingers twisting in the bedsheets.

"Every night," he said, his voice dropping to that delicious register that made my thighs clench, "I lie here thinking about what I want to do to you. What I want you to do to me."

He hooked his thumbs in the waistband of his boxer briefs, hesitating for just a moment before slowly sliding them down. My breath caught as he revealed himself fully—thick, hard, and perfect. I couldn't look away.

I watched, mesmerized, as he began to stroke himself slowly. His hand moved with practiced ease, twisting slightly at the head before sliding back down. His eyes never left me, intense and burning with desire. The muscles in his arm flexed with each movement, his breathing growing heavier. A soft whimper escaped me, and I shifted on the bed, suddenly aware of how wet I was just from watching him.

"I lie in this bed thinking about you. About how you felt under my hands. How you taste."

His voice was a low, sensual rumble that sent shivers down my spine. Watching him touch himself while thinking of me was the most erotic thing I'd ever witnessed.

A low moan escaped my lips before I could stop it. The sound seemed to affect him instantly—his hand moved faster, his breathing growing ragged as a bead of moisture formed at his tip.

"Your turn Liz," he rasped. "Show me what I do to you."

His words sent a thrill through me. My hands trembled as I reached for the zipper of my hoodie, slowly pulling it down. The sound seemed impossibly loud in the quiet room. I shrugged it off, letting it fall to the floor, revealing the simple tank top underneath.

"Keep going," Brett encouraged. The raw need in his voice set my body on fire. His hand never stopped moving on his length, his eyes burning into mine.

I crossed my arms, grabbing the hem of my tank top and pulling it over my head. The cool air kissed my skin, making my nipples tighten against the thin fabric of my bra. I heard Brett's sharp intake of breath, saw the way his hand faltered for just a moment.

"I think about you too," I admitted, my voice barely above a whisper. "Every night."

I stood, my fingers trembling slightly as pushed my leggings down my legs. Brett's hand slowed on himself as he watched me, his chest rising and falling with each heavy breath. The intensity of his gaze made me feel powerful, desired in a way I'd never experienced before.

"God, you're beautiful," he whispered.

My cheeks flushed with heat, but I didn't look away.

Reaching behind me, I unhooked my bra with trembling fingers, letting it slide down my arms. Brett's eyes darkened as he took in the sight of my bare breasts, his hand tightening around himself.

"Touch yourself," he commanded softly. "Show me what you do when you think about me."

I sat back on the edge of the bed, my heart hammering against my ribs. Slowly, I slid one hand down my stomach, past the waistband of my underwear. A soft moan escaped me as my fingers found the slick heat between my thighs.

"That's it," Brett encouraged, his voice strained. "Let me see what I do to you."

I circled my clit with my fingers, my hips lifting slightly off the bed. The intensity of his gaze on me was almost too much to bear. With my free hand, I cupped my breast, pinching my nipple between my fingers as I continued to stroke myself. Brett's breathing grew ragged, his hand moving faster on his length.

"I can't take this anymore," Brett said suddenly, his voice strained. "I need to touch you."

"Yes," I gasped, withdrawing my hand. "Please."

In an instant, he was kneeling between my legs, his hands sliding up my thighs. He hooked his fingers into my underwear and pulled them down with an urgency that made me shiver. Then his mouth was on me, hot and demanding against my core, and I cried out, my back arching off the bed. His tongue was relentless, licking, circling, tasting me with an intensity that stole my breath.

"Brett," I gasped, my fingers tangling in his hair. "Oh god."

His hands gripped my thighs, holding me open for him as he devoured me like a man starved. Each stroke of his tongue brought me closer to the edge, my hips rocking against his mouth of their own accord.

"You taste even better than I remembered," he murmured against my sensitive flesh, his breath hot and teasing.

I was already so close, wound tight from watching him touch himself.

When he slid two fingers inside me while his tongue continued its relentless assault on my clit, I shattered, crying out his name as waves of pleasure crashed through me. My thighs trembled around his head, my body pulsing with aftershocks as he gentled his touch, placing soft kisses on my inner thighs.

"I'm not done with you yet," he murmured, rising to hover above me. His eyes were dark with need, his lips glistening with evidence of my pleasure. "I want to be inside you, Liz. I need to feel you."

"Yes," I breathed, reaching for him. "Please, Brett."

He moved away from me for just a moment, reaching toward his nightstand. I watched, breathless and impatient, as he yanked open the drawer and pulled out a small foil packet. My heart thundered in my chest as he tore it open with his teeth—a move that shouldn't have been as sexy as it was, but God, everything about this man was devastating.

His hands were steady but urgent as he rolled the condom down his length. I couldn't look away from the fluid motion, the controlled power in his fingers, the intensity in his expression. There was something incredibly intimate about watching him prepare like this—practical, necessary, but somehow one of the sexiest things I'd ever seen.

"I've thought about this," I whispered, propping myself up on my elbows. "About you. Inside me."

His eyes darkened at my words, pupils blown wide with desire.

"Tell me," he rasped, positioning himself between my thighs, the blunt head of his cock pressing against my entrance. "Tell me exactly what you imagined."

I trembled, both from anticipation and the vulnerability of confession. "I imagined you fucking me. Hard. Deep. Fast."

His eyes flashed with heat as he slowly pushed forward, stretching me, filling me inch by delicious inch until I gasped, my back arching off the bed.

"Like this?" he growled, withdrawing almost completely before driving back in with a powerful thrust that made me cry out.

"Yes," I panted, my fingers digging into his shoulders. "Just like that."

Brett set a relentless pace, his hips snapping against mine with each powerful thrust. Every stroke hit something deep inside me that made stars explode behind my eyelids. I wrapped my legs around his waist, pulling him even deeper, wanting—needing—more of him.

"You feel incredible," he murmured, his voice strained with the effort. "So tight. So perfect."

"More," I gasped, my nails raking down his back. "Harder."

Something primal flashed in his eyes. In one fluid motion, he flipped me over, his hands gripping my hips as he positioned me on my knees in front of him.

The new position left me feeling deliciously exposed, vulnerable in a way that sent electric currents of anticipation through my body.

"Is this what you want?" he murmured, his voice rough with desire. "Tell me, Liz."

"Yes," I breathed, pushing back against him impatiently. "Please, Brett."

He groaned, one hand sliding beneath me to cup my breast while the other gripped my hip. I felt him position himself at my entrance, teasing me with just the tip until I whimpered with need.

"Look at you," he said, his voice filled with wonder. "So perfect. So beautiful."

I couldn't respond, could barely breathe as he began to move. Each thrust was deeper than before, hitting places inside me that made coherent thought impossible. The sound of skin against skin, our mingled breaths and moans filled the room as he took me with an intensity that bordered on worship.

One of his hands slid up my spine, tangling in my hair and pulling gently, arching my back even more. The slight sting sent a jolt of pleasure straight to my core, making me cry out with a mixture of pleasure and surprise.

"You like that?" he murmured, his voice dark with satisfaction.

"Yes," I gasped, pushing back against him, meeting each thrust with an eagerness that surprised even me. "Don't stop."

His rhythm became more urgent, more demanding, and I knew he was close. My fingers found my clit again, circling with just the right pressure as he continued to drive into me.

The dual sensation was overwhelming, pushing me rapidly toward the edge.

"Come for me, Liz," he commanded, his voice rough with need. "I want to feel you come around my cock."

His words were all it took. I shattered, crying out his name as waves of pleasure crashed through me, my body clenching around him in pulsing waves. He groaned, his rhythm faltering as my release triggered his own. His fingers dug into my hips as he held me tight against him, his body shuddering as he found his release.

We collapsed onto the bed together, a tangle of limbs and racing heartbeats. Brett pulled me against his chest, his arms wrapping around me with a tenderness that made my heart ache. I could feel his heart hammering against my back, his breath warm against my neck as we both struggled to regain control.

"That put my imagination to shame," Brett murmured against my hair, placing a soft kiss on my shoulder.

I laughed softly, the sound warm and languid in the afterglow. "Mine too."

For several minutes, we just breathed together, my back against his chest, his heartbeat steadying against my spine. His fingers traced lazy patterns on my skin, sending little shivers of pleasure through me even now.

"Stay," he whispered, pressing a soft kiss to my shoulder. Not a question. Not quite a command. Something in between—hopeful and certain all at once.

I turned in his arms to face him, taking in the vulnerability in his eyes. "Just tonight?"

His expression softened, a smile playing at the corners of his mouth. "Tonight. Tomorrow. As long as you want."

My heart stuttered. "That could be a while."

"I'm counting on it," he said, a slow smile spreading across his face as he brushed a strand of hair from my cheek.

I nestled closer, my body still humming with lingering pleasure. "Be careful what you wish for, Wentworth. I've been told I'm stubborn."

"Good," he murmured, pressing a kiss to my forehead. "Because I'm not going anywhere."

His words settled around me like a blanket, warm and secure. For once, I didn't feel the need to overthink or analyze. I just wanted to be here, in this moment, with him.

Epilogue

BRETT

IN MY DEFENSE, I'VE handled high-stakes investor meetings, near-hostile board takeovers, and one deeply terrifying Mia-pitch involving glitter cannons.

But nothing—*nothing*—prepared me for Liz waking me up at 3:41 a.m. with the words: "Either my water broke, or I peed myself—jury's still out."

I, of course, responded like a calm, capable partner.

By tripping over the hospital bag, grabbing the car keys off the nightstand, and yelling into my phone, "She's leaking something! How do I install a car seat in less than thirty seconds?"

"You had nine months—"

"Logan!"

"Okay, okay. Stay calm. Do *not* try to YouTube anything right now."

"Too late. I already tried YouTube and now I'm being yelled at by a British man named Nigel!"

Meanwhile, Liz slid into the passenger seat, casually on the phone like we weren't mid-emergency. "I'm having the baby," she said to Mia. "No, I'm calm. Brett's the one spiraling."

In my defense, I was not spiraling.

From the background, I heard Mia shout, "TELL HIM TO HURRY. I HAVE SNACKS AND A T-SHIRT THAT SAYS I DESIGNED THE BABY!"

We made it to the hospital. Liz cursed like a sailor the entire drive. I may or may not have cried when they put the little squirmy, furious bundle in my arms six hours later.

She was perfect. Small. Strong. Loud—like her mom.

Liz, exhausted but somehow still sharp, gave me a crooked smile from the bed.

"You didn't faint."

"I'm saving that for when she brings home her first boyfriend."

From the hallway, Mia's voice rang out. "If you name her Epson, I am leaving this family."

I looked back at Liz. Her hair was a mess, her hospital gown was wrinkled and slipping off one shoulder, and I had never seen anyone so beautiful.

"You still hate me?" I whispered, kissing her cheek.

"Only when you leave the toilet seat up. And maybe when you hog the covers."

Fair enough.

Tempting Mr. Dawson

A Spicy, Mistaken-Identity Billionaire Romcom with a Flirty Twist of Tropical Heat

Hana York

Pink Pop Publishing

Tempting Mr. Dawson

(Don't Fall for the Billionaire Book 2)

Copyright © 2025 by Hana York

www.HanaYork.com

Contents

Chapter One

PIPER

IF ONE MORE PERSON offered me a coconut drink adorned with a paper umbrella, I was going to find a creative new place to stick that umbrella.

I hadn't endured three connecting flights, two tedious layovers, and a skeptical customs agent questioning if 'Piper' was really my name, just to lounge by the pool sipping Piña coladas.

Don't misunderstand me—the place was breathtaking. Towering palms swayed majestically, the air was perfumed with the intoxicating scent of hibiscus, and the vistas were so mesmerizing they could make you forget your Wi-Fi password. But it all felt... unnervingly perfect. Like the resort had been airbrushed by an influencer with a lucrative brand deal.

I wasn't here for that glossy façade. I came for the real story. I sought the authentic narrative—the imperfections, the untold stories behind the scenes, the people who kept this paradise running. Not the glossy brochure version.

"Miss Winslow?" A woman in crisp linen handed me a refreshingly cold towel—much appreciated after a thirty-minute cab ride full of flirty winks and zero road signs.

I took it with a polite smile and patted my neck. 'Thanks. Definitely hits the spot.

Was it weird to hope they had cold towels for emotional baggage too? Asking for a friend. (Me. I'm the friend.)

She beamed and gestured toward the open-air lobby. "Your room will be ready shortly. In the meantime, feel free to explore the grounds. Or enjoy a welcome cocktail by the pool."

There it was. Coconut drink number three.

I wandered toward the water, mentally drafting the opening lines of my article—*There's luxury, and then there's curated illusion. The Coral Bay Resort promises both.*

And then my brain hit a full stop.

Directly ahead of me, a guy was adjusting a poolside umbrella. Tall, broad-shouldered, with forearms that should've come with a warning label, he wore a bright Hawaiian shirt and khakis that screamed, *I work here, but I could easily moonlight as an underwear model.*

He grunted as he lifted the umbrella, and an uninvited burst of heat shot straight to my core.

How rude.

As if he could feel me staring—and to be fair, I was—he turned.

And wow.

Square jaw. Scruff. Laugh lines. The kind of face that probably called people *darlin'* and got away with it.

Great. Now the staff were hot. Like, *seriously* hot.

I spun toward the nearest palm tree and stared at it like I was contemplating photosynthesis.

Smooth, Piper. Nailed it.

Too late. He was already walking over, smile set to *charm with a side of trouble*.

"If you're hoping that one's going to whisper the meaning of life," he said, "you've picked the wrong palm."

I looked back at him, mouth going dry. And yes, I clocked the broad chest, the undone buttons, the criminally attractive everything—but it was the crinkles around his eyes that hit hardest.

Unfair.

"Actually, I'm a palm tree expert," I said, crossing my arms. "This one's warning me about men in Hawaiian shirts who get a little too confident about crooked umbrellas."

His laugh was low and genuine—none of the rehearsed charm I was starting to expect around here.

"Smart tree," he said, still grinning.

"I'm Logan," he added, extending a hand.

I took it—firm, callused, warm. Definitely not just supervisory.

"Piper."

"Nice to meet you, Piper. You settling in?"

"I'm three coconut drinks in and already bonded with a gecko that might know my deepest secrets. So... I'd say things are going well."

He chuckled. "That'd be Tito. He thinks he runs the place."

"You're not going to argue?"

"Nope. He's earned it."

And then he laughed—and, of course, it was the kind of laugh that made me feel warm in places that were none of his business.

"Well," I said, backing up a step before I asked him to fix *my* umbrella, "thanks for the unofficial welcome."

"Anytime," he said—somehow, it felt like a promise.

LOGAN

She didn't recognize me.

That was the first thing I noticed as she walked off—hips swinging, like she knew exactly what kind of distraction she was and didn't mind one bit. No double take. No polite curiosity. Just a once-over and the kind of breezy dismissal I hadn't gotten in years.

Honestly? Kind of refreshing.

It usually doesn't take long for people to figure out who I am. Not because I'm famous, but when your name's tied to the company, staff tend to straighten up fast. Guests too, once they catch on.

But Piper—just Piper, because that's all she gave me—had absolutely no idea she'd just sass-smiled the CEO of Coral Bay Resorts.

Even better? She'd critiqued my umbrella skills and insulted my shirt in the same breath. And I was hooked.

I adjusted another umbrella—reflex—and watched her settle into a lounger like it was second nature. No phone. Just a notebook. She flipped it open, scribbled something, then tapped the pen against her lips like the ficus next to her was feeding her plot points.

Definitely not a tourist.

"Sir?" Steve, the *actual* pool attendant, appeared beside me, looking concerned. "Do you, uh... need help with something?"

I kept my gaze on her. "Just checking on things."

Steve hovered, clearly torn between questioning my sanity and slowly backing away. He followed my line of sight.

"That guest," I said. "With the notebook. Who is she?"

"Oh, Ms. Winslow." He straightened a little, like remembering her name earned him points. "She's the travel writer Mr. Daniels coordinated with PR. Full-access. Three-week stay. Wanderlust Magazine."

Of course.

Piper Winslow. The writer my team had been buzzing about for months. The same one who called the Bellagio's "oppressive scent branding" a "designer migraine in disguise." Who'd tanked a five-star eco-resort by describing their composting program as *composting my will to live*.

A travel writer whose words could murder a hotel in under 800 characters.

And here I was, trying to flirt with her in a pineapple-print shirt.

She scribbled something else into her notebook, then gave the pool bar a look that said, "*Interesting choice*," with just enough attitude to make me want to defend the barstools.

Definitely not what I expected. PR said she was sharp and established, which I had translated as *cynical, mid-forties, maybe allergic to joy.*

But Piper? She was young. Witty. Slightly terrifying. And clearly not here to fall for curated charm.

Well. Shit.

Now, I kind of wanted to know what she'd write about me.

Chapter Two

PIPER

THE CORAL BAY RESORT was a journalist's paradise. Not because of the white sand beaches or the infinity pool that looked like it was designed to capture every last ray of sunshine, but because there was a story lurking beneath every perfectly arranged orchid.

I stared at my notebook, tapping my pen against the page where I'd scribbled *Hawaiian shirt—too many buttons undone* and then immediately crossed it out.

Not relevant to the article. *At all*.

"Focus, Piper," I muttered. I was here to investigate whether Coral Bay lived up to its eco-conscious promises—or if it was just another greenwashed playground for people who flew private and called it carbon-neutral because they brought reusable water bottles.

Not to ogle the guy with forearms that should require a permit and a laugh that had no business being that warm.

I forced my focus back to the setting. The resort was undeniably beautiful—all natural materials, and not a plastic straw in sight. Even the pool towels were rolled like they'd been arranged by a very calm monk.

But I wasn't here to be dazzled.

I was here to dig, to find the tiny tells—cheap finishes passed off as artisanal, imported produce labeled local, spa products "inspired by nature" that came in non-recyclable packaging, the cracks in the shine, the gap between the marketing and the truth.

My phone pinged. A message from the front desk: *Your suite is ready, Ms. Winslow. Welcome again to Coral Bay.*

Perfect. I could use a change—these clothes had survived three flights, two layovers, and one nap on my carry-on. It was barely 10 am, and they'd already earned their retirement.

Fifteen minutes later, I was standing in a suite that could make an Instagram influencer cry tears of aesthetic joy. Floor-to-ceiling windows framed the ocean like a living painting. The bed was covered in what had to be 1200-thread-count sheets. Even the complimentary slippers looked like they came with their own trust funds.

I stepped onto the balcony, letting the warm, salty breeze wash over me.

And then I spotted him.

Down by the pool, umbrella guy, Logan, was laughing with another member of the staff. He gestured animatedly with one hand like he was telling some ridiculous story, which made the guy beside him double over in laughter.

I couldn't tear my eyes away from him. There was something about the way he moved—confident but not cocky, like a man who knew exactly how much space he occupied in the world and was comfortable with it. His shoulders shifted beneath that ridiculous Hawaiian shirt as he gestured, and I wondered what they'd look like without it. Probably sculpted. Probably tanned. Probably the kind of shoulders that made intelligent women forget how to form complete sentences.

What was wrong with me? I was here on assignment, not to mentally undress the staff.

But there was something magnetic about him. The way his laugh carried across the distance, the casual grace with which he leaned against the bar, the way his hands moved when he talked... I found myself wondering what those hands would feel like—against my skin, in my hair, gripping my hips.

I inhaled sharply, stepping back from the railing.

Three weeks. I had three weeks to write this piece, and I couldn't afford to spend them fantasizing about some resort employee, no matter how unfairly attractive he was.

"Get it together, Winslow," I muttered, turning away from the balcony and back into my suite. I needed to unpack, shower, and get my head on straight.

I took a long, steadying breath. I'd been on the road too long—three back-to-back assignments before this one. That had to be why I was fixating on a random hotel employee with a nice smile. Professional burnout manifesting as inappropriate attraction. That was definitely a thing, right?

Absolutely, I decided.

I unpacked quickly, tossing my clothes into the drawers without much thought, eager to get to my shower. I unfastened my jeans and shimmied out of them, tossing them over the back of a chair. My tank top followed. I unhooked my bra and let it drop to the floor, then slid out of my panties, leaving a trail of travel exhaustion in my wake as I padded into the bathroom. The water was already running, steam beginning to fog the glass. I stepped toward the shower, one foot in—

And someone knocked.

I froze.

Housekeeping, probably.

"Just a sec!" I called, grabbing the robe off the hook by the bathroom door. I yanked it on haphazardly, not bothering to tighten the belt.

I opened the door with zero hesitation—and even less robe security.

And instantly regretted all my life choices.

Because it wasn't housekeeping.

It was Logan.

Clipboard in one hand, he stood there with that confident, effortless stance. His gaze dipped, barely a beat, but it was enough to make me painfully aware that my robe was one good exhale away from complete betrayal.

LOGAN

I'm sure there's a management seminar somewhere about this exact scenario. *What Not to Do When Meeting the Travel Writer Who Could Destroy Your Company: A CEO's Guide.*

Slide one: Don't stand frozen in her doorway while she's practically naked.

But holy hell.

Piper Winslow stood there in a hotel robe that was doing the absolute minimum of its job. One shoulder was nearly exposed, and the belt was loose enough to reveal the shadow between her breasts.

Her eyes widened, recognition flickering. "Hawaiian shirt guy."

"Logan," I said, voice embarrassingly rough. "From the... umbrella incident."

"Right." She clutched the robe tighter, which somehow made everything worse. "Did you get promoted to room service in the last hour?"

"No. I just wanted to catch you before your schedule filled up."

I lifted the clipboard like it might protect me from the very real threat of her bare skin. "Thought you might like a personal tour. Behind the scenes. Off the brochure. Figured it'd be more useful than another coconut cocktail."

Her brows lifted. For a second, I thought she'd laugh me out of the hallway. But then her expression shifted. Curious. Cautious. Maybe a little intrigued.

"A personal tour?" She leaned against the doorframe, the robe shifting just enough to make my brain short-circuit. "From the pool attendant?"

Perfect moment to tell her the truth. That I wasn't just Logan with the umbrellas and the shirts. That I owned the damn place.

But I didn't.

Because she wasn't looking at me like a CEO. She wasn't calculating, deferential or guarded. She was looking at me like I was a person.

"I know the place better than most," I said instead. True. "Every corner, every hidden spot. The stuff they don't show in the promo videos." I tapped the clipboard. "No PR script. No staged photo ops. Just the real story."

She studied me. Her gaze was sharp like she was trying to slice through whatever performance I might be giving.

"And why would you do that? Out of the goodness of your heart?"

I grinned. "Maybe I just want Wanderlust Magazine to get the full picture."

Her eyes narrowed. "How do you know I'm with Wanderlust?"

Shit. Shit. *Shit.*

"Small resort. Word travels fast." I kept my tone easy, trying to recover. "Especially when someone interesting checks in."

Still skeptical, but the edge softened. "Interesting, huh?"

"Most guests don't psychoanalyze palm trees."

A reluctant smile. "Fair enough." She adjusted the robe again. My eyes did not get the memo to look away.

"So when's this mysterious off-brochure tour happening? I was about to shower."

Yeah. I'd noticed.

"Half an hour?" I managed. "Gives you time to, uh... do whatever you were doing."

She raised one brow. I nearly tripped over my own tongue.

"Shower," she clarified, dry as hell.

"Right. Yes. That."

"Forty-five minutes," she countered. "I need to wash off three airports."

I nodded, trying not to picture her in the shower. Failing spectacularly. "I'll meet you in the lobby."

"By the koi pond with the judgmental fish?" she asked.

"You've met them already?"

"The orange one gave me a look when I dropped my sunglasses."

I laughed. "That's Mochi. He judges everyone."

"You named the fish?"

"Of course." I tried not to stare at the smooth curve of her neck. "Every good resort has named fish. It's in the handbook."

She laughed—and God, the sound was all warmth and trouble. "Let me guess. You're the resort's resident eccentric?"

"Something like that." I stepped back before I could make things worse. "Forty-five minutes. Koi pond."

"It's a date," she said—then immediately flushed. "I mean—not a date-date. A professional thing."

"Professional thing," I echoed. "Got it."

The second her door clicked shut, I leaned against the wall, dragging a hand down my face.

My heart raced like I'd just run a 10K in sand.

I loosened another button on my shirt, then immediately regretted it when an older couple passed and gave me a look.

Great. Logan Dawson: resort mogul, acting like a flustered teenager.

Forty-five minutes.

Which meant right now—this very second—Piper Winslow was in the shower. Water streaming down her body. Steam curling around her skin.

"For the love of all that is holy," I muttered, pushing off the wall and speed-walking toward the elevator like the devil was chasing me.

Inside, I jammed the clipboard against my crotch like it was my last line of defense. And at this point, it was.

"This is ridiculous," I hissed. "You're forty. Not fourteen."

I tried thinking about spreadsheets. Board meeting. Anything that didn't involve Piper naked and wet.

Didn't work.

The elevator opened. I made a beeline for my office, dodging staff like a man on a mission.

"Mr. Dawson, I have those—"

"Later," I barked, slamming my door behind me.

This was absurd. I had a company to run, investors to placate, and a magazine profile hanging in the balance.

And all I could think about was the curve of her hip in that damn robe.

Forty-two minutes.

"Think about the shareholders," I muttered. "Think about quarterly reports. Think about anything besides Piper Winslow in a steamy rainforest fantasy."

Nope. My brain had its own agenda. And it involved a very naked, very wet Piper.

Thirty-eight minutes.

This was untenable.

I stalked into my private bathroom, locked the door, unbuckled my belt, and gave in.

I gripped myself hard, already fully erect from the mental images that had been torturing me.

My hand moved furiously as I leaned against the cool marble countertop, my breathing ragged and uneven.

"Fuck," I hissed through clenched teeth.

My pace quickened, my hand a blur. The pressure built almost immediately, my body wound so tight from frustration that release was already imminent.

The tension coiled impossibly tight before snapping. My release hit with staggering force, my entire body shuddering as waves of pleasure ripped through me. I braced myself against the counter with my free hand, knees nearly buckling as I rode out the intensity of it.

"Piper," I groaned, my voice barely recognizable.

For several moments I just stood there, breathing hard, reality slowly returning. My legs felt weak, my pulse pounding in my ears like a bass drum.

This was insane. I hadn't lost control like that since... well, ever.

"Thirty-one minutes," I muttered, glancing at my watch as I cleaned myself up.

I washed my hands, splashed cold water on my face, and stared at my reflection. The man in the mirror looked slightly less unhinged now. I smoothed my hair, adjusted my shirt, and took a deep breath.

"You're playing with fire," I told my reflection.

Chapter Three

PIPER

I slammed the door shut and leaned against it, heart thudding like I'd just outrun a charging bull.

"What. The. Actual. Hell."

I stared at my reflection in the mirror by the door. Flushed cheeks, tangled hair, eyes too wide and bright. I looked... affected. By a man in a Hawaiian shirt who adjusted umbrellas for a living.

"You're here to work," I told myself sternly. "Not to flirt. Definitely not to drool."

I stepped into the shower, hot water pouring over my travel-weary body—but Logan's voice echoed in my mind. Rough, low, like it had brushed against gravel when he said my name. And those hands. Big, capable, confident hands. The kind that could wreak havoc on my senses—and my body.

"Stop it," I groaned, lathering shampoo, hoping it would wash away my thoughts.

This was ridiculous. I'd known the man for five minutes, and my brain was writing him into very inappropriate chapters of my life.

But when my fingers grazed my breasts, slick with suds, a bolt of heat arrowed straight through me. God, it had been a while. Too long.

"Just to take the edge off," I muttered, letting one hand slide lower. My breath hitched as I found myself already aching, already there.

I leaned against the tile, eyes slipping closed. In my mind, Logan stepped into the shower behind me. No Hawaiian shirt. Just heat and skin and hands that knew exactly what they were doing. His mouth at my ear, teasing. Then lower.

The fantasy took hold fast—Logan lifting me like I weighed nothing, pinning me to the wall, making me feel things I had no business feeling for a man I just met.

"Oh shit," I gasped, climax hitting hard and fast, stealing my breath and the last of my control. I slumped against the wall, letting the water rinse away the evidence.

Real professional, Winslow.

When I could stand without wobbling, I toweled off and dressed slowly and deliberately. I wore a breezy, professional-ish sundress. I put on a little mascara and some lip balm, just enough polish to say *competent journalist,* not *woman who had just had a fantasy-fueled meltdown in the shower.*

"You've got this," I told the mirror. "Just a tour. A behind-the-scenes look. For work."

My reflection raised an eyebrow at me like, *sure thing, Piper.*

Notebook in hand, I made my way down to the koi pond with what I hoped was professional poise and not just carefully choreographed denial.

Logan was already there, crouched by the water, trailing his fingers through the surface as koi swam lazy circles around him. His profile was annoyingly perfect—jaw carved from granite, stubble in all the right places, hair rumpled like he'd been running hands through it. A lot.

He hadn't seen me yet, which gave me the chance to just... look. So I did. And yeah, the Hawaiian shirt was still ridiculous, four buttons undone Magnum PI style, but it somehow worked on him.

I cleared my throat.

He looked up—and when he smiled, it was like the sun stretched just a little closer to earth.

"Right on time," he said, rising to his full height.

Had he always been that tall? Because suddenly I felt small. And not in a bad way.

Not in a bad way at all.

LOGAN

She tilted her head, notebook in one hand, lips curved like she couldn't decide if she was impressed or suspicious. Probably both.

"Lead the way, umbrella guy."

God help me, I liked the way she said that.

I led her toward the beach, where a pair of paddleboards waited near the water sports hut.

"Paddleboarding?" she asked, eyeing the boards suspiciously.

"Gentle ocean tour," I said. "Standing optional. Dignity not guaranteed."

She gave me a flat look. "Wow. What a sell."

"You want the glossy brochure or the real deal?"

With a theatrical sigh, she kicked off her sandals. "Fine. But if I end up face-down in the Pacific, I'm titling the article *'Local Umbrella Guy Endangers Award-Winning Journalist'.*"

"I'll make you a plaque." I offered with a chuckle.

She rolled her eyes—then, in one smooth, merciless motion, reached for the hem of her sundress and pulled it over her head.

And I forgot how to breathe.

The bikini was simple, black, efficient, and somehow hotter than lace and strappy nonsense. Her skin glowed in the sun, golden and warm, and when she bent to tuck her dress and sandals into a nearby cubby, I got a flash of long legs and the curve of her ass—perfectly framed by that bikini.

Focus. Ocean. Boards. Breathing.

She turned and caught me looking. Because, of course, she did.

"Eyes up, guest services," she said flatly.

I cleared my throat. "Just checking for SPF compliance. Can't have you burning on my watch."

"Mmm." She smirked. "Very dedicated to guest wellness."

And then she stepped onto her board like she was born doing it—knees bent, balance perfect, arms relaxed. Off she went, skimming across the water like she had a personal relationship with Poseidon.

I followed, doing my best to look cool. I was doing fine. Mostly. Until she turned her head, gave me that smug little smile.

That's when the ocean betrayed me.

One wobble, then another. I tried to recover, then splash. Down I went. Full bellyflop.

When I surfaced, she was laughing so hard she had to clutch her board for support.

"Are you okay?" she called, breathless with amusement.

"Totally fine," I said, spitting out salt water. "This is just part of the immersive experience."

She grinned, wide and wicked. "Authentic. I like it."

"I suffer for my guests' content."

"You might want to rethink that," she teased. "I'm ruthless in my reviews."

"Duly noted." I hauled myself back onto my board. "Remind me to take you to Jellyfish Lagoon next."

Still laughing, she paddled beside me as we drifted toward the shore. Her hair curled wildly in the heat, her skin glistening, her eyes dancing.

"You really committed to the fall," she said, handing me a towel as we came ashore.

"Well, someone had to entertain the fish," I said, toweling off.

She let out a laugh—unguarded and honest. It punched straight through my ribs and lodged itself somewhere inconvenient.

"Please tell me the next stop doesn't involve balance or core strength," she said, slipping her sundress over her swimsuit again.

I pretended to think. "Define 'core strength'."

Her eyes narrowed. "Not encouraging."

I tipped my head toward a shaded pavilion at the beach's edge. The air smelled like lime, garlic, and open flame. A small crowd gathered around prep tables stacked with fruit, herbs, and knives.

"Pop-up cooking class," I said casually. "Local chef. Fresh ingredients. Very hands-on."

"You're taking me to chop things?"

"It's a bonding exercise," I said. "Like paddleboarding. But with knives."

"Fantastic," she muttered. "Nothing says vacation like potential blood loss."

Still, she followed.

The chef welcomed us with a thick accent and a sharp blade, launching into a rapid-fire description of what we'd be making—something with mango, jalapeño, lime, and a level of enthusiasm that suggested danger.

Piper stared down at her cutting board like it had personally offended her.

"Relax," I said, tossing her a pair of gloves. "It's just fruit salad. With ambition."

She glanced sideways. "Okay, no. How are you that fast?"

I shrugged, already halfway through my second mango. "I've made this before."

"You've made tropical ceviche?"

"I've made a lot of things."

She squinted at me. "You're suspiciously competent for someone who looks like he moonlights in underwear ads."

I grinned. "So you think I look like an underwear model."

"That is not what I said."

"Pretty sure it is."

She pointed her knife at me. "Chop more. Talk less."

I raised an eyebrow. "You're threatening me with a knife? Bold move."

"If you so much as smile, I'll turn this mango into a weapon."

I laughed, and she quickly refocused on her board, her lips pressed together, probably trying not to smile.

But yeah.

That one was definitely going into the memory bank.

Chapter Four

PIPER

I DIDN'T *MEAN* TO say he looked like an underwear model. It just... slipped out like a rogue truth launching out of my mouth before my brain could tackle it.

And Logan grinned like he'd just won something.

I dropped my gaze and focused on the task at hand, determined to make at least one cube-shaped thing before looking up again. When I finally snuck a peek, his cutting board looked like a gourmet magazine cover. Mine, on the other hand, looked like a crime scene.

The chef shouted something rapid-fire, and Logan slid a small tasting bowl before me.

"You're up, journalist," he said. "Taste and judge."

I dipped my spoon, tasted, and—damn it. Bright, spicy, citrusy... annoyingly perfect.

I kept my expression neutral. "Eh. Needs more salt."

His brow arched. "Liar."

Before I could think better of it, I grabbed a clean slice of mango, scooped a bit of ceviche onto it, and held it out to him.

He leaned in, eyes locked on mine—and took the bite from my fingers, slow as sin. His lips brushed my fingertips.

And then—dear *God*—he licked them.

The lightest swipe of his tongue against my fingertips, just enough to melt every coherent thought I had.

My breath hitched. I squeezed my thighs together like that might short-circuit the heat building there. It didn't help. In fact, it made everything *worse*.

"Needs more salt, huh?" he murmured, voice deliciously low.

I swallowed hard. "On second thought, it's... adequate."

"Adequate?" His eyes crinkled. "That's the best you can do?"

"Fine," I muttered. "It's delicious. Happy now?"

"Ecstatic," he said, still way too pleased with himself. "For a writer, you're shockingly stingy with compliments."

I needed air. Which was ironic, considering we were literally *outside*.

"I, uh…" I cleared my throat and stepped back. "Need a break. That jalapeño is no joke."

Logan tilted his head, one brow raised like he saw straight through me. But instead of pushing, he grabbed two bottles of water from a nearby cooler and offered me one.

"Come on," he said. "There's a local market down by the east beach. No lime juice. Minimal chopping."

I nodded, clutching the bottle like hydration might solve my… situation.

We strolled along a shaded path, palm leaves rustling overhead, the ocean humming somewhere beyond the trees. I risked a glance at him—relaxed, casual like he hadn't just set my nerve endings on fire.

Totally unfair.

The market appeared around a bend—half a dozen colorful stalls under fluttering fabric canopies, bursting with handmade baskets, carved trinkets, shell jewelry, and tiny jars of mango chili jam.

It was charming. Breezy. Exactly what I needed.

We wandered in companionable silence. I drifted between booths, pretending I was 100% focused on artisanal crafts and not thinking about Logan's mouth on my fingers.

Focus. Necklaces. Local culture. Not how he smelled like sunscreen and sin.

He stopped at a small table tucked into the corner, shaded by frayed linen. An older woman sat behind it, long silver braid over one shoulder, eyes sparkling like she *knew things*.

"Ah," she said, voice warm and confident. "You've found the love charms."

I blinked. "The what now?"

She held up two delicate shell bracelets, pale pink and cream, threaded onto soft leather. "For soul-tied lovers. Very rare shells. They wash up together."

I opened my mouth to politely decline, but Logan spoke first. "That's beautiful," he said, his voice low and sincere.

Before I could respond, she tied one around my wrist with practiced hands—gentle but firm. Then she did the same to him.

"You wear them," she said, smiling at both of us, "to remember that real love doesn't question. It recognizes."

We stood there like awkward teenagers, neither of us speaking.

Finally, Logan cleared his throat. "How much do we owe you?"

She waved him off like he'd offended her deeply. "They already belong to you."

We murmured awkward thank-yous and walked off slowly. The silence between us suddenly charged.

"She thinks we're..." I trailed off.

"Yeah," Logan said. "Caught that."

"She was *very* confident."

He glanced at his bracelet, then at me, considering. "Well, I have a rule not to argue with women who could probably hex me with a coconut."

I laughed. "Wise."

We kept walking, the market noise fading behind us. The path narrowed again, shaded and quiet except for the occasional birdcall and the squeak of my sandals.

I didn't know where we were going.

But I didn't ask.

LOGAN

Piper didn't ask where we were going. Just walked beside me, quiet but comfortable, her fingers brushing the shell bracelet like she couldn't decide how she felt about it.

Honestly? Same.

We turned down a shaded alley lined with hanging plants and crooked stone pavers, and I led us to a tiny café tucked between a pottery studio and a wind chime shop made entirely of old wine bottles. No sign. No name. Just the smell of roasted coffee and banana bread so good it might convince you to believe in miracles.

Her eyes lit up. "This is nice."

"Locals swear by it," I said. "Best caffeine and carbs on the island."

We ordered two iced coffees and a slice of banana bread she *claimed* she didn't want—but somehow managed to eat more than half of. I didn't say a word. I'm no rookie.

We tucked into a corner table beneath a crooked ceiling fan, the kind that looked like it had seen some things. For a minute, we just sipped in silence.

It felt good. Uncomplicated.

I took a long drink of coffee, then asked, "You ever get tired of it?"

She looked up. "Tired of what?"

"The job. Constant travel. New faces. New lobbies. Same questions."

She studied me like she was trying to decide whether I was making polite conversation or actually curious.

"The travel part? No," she said. "The small talk, the hotel lobbies that all smell like someone sprayed lemon Pledge, the 'let me show you our signature cocktail' speeches while I'm hallucinating from time zone jet lag? Yeah. That gets old."

There was something practiced in how she said it—like it wasn't the first time.

I paused, then asked, "What about your family?"

That earned a short, dry laugh. "Oh, going straight for the heavy hitters."

"You don't have to answer."

"No, it's okay. Just funny. Most people open with favorite color or pizza toppings."

I raised a brow. "Want to talk pizza toppings? I can talk pizza toppings. Though I'm guessing yours is something criminal like anchovies."

She gave me a smirk. "Pineapple."

"Borderline unforgivable."

She snorted into her iced coffee and leaned back. "Okay. Family. I've got a mom. No siblings. Just me and the queen of serial marriage."

"How serial?"

"She's on husband number seven."

I blinked. "Seven?"

"Lucky number, apparently. She insists it's always true love. Soulmates, she says."

I raised an eyebrow. "Soulmate of the month?"

Her smile tightened. "Pretty much. I'm starting to think she collects husbands like some people collect wine."

Logan grinned. "So, she's on husband number seven and still believes in soulmates?"

"Exactly." Piper's smile faded a little. "Watching her rotate husbands like seasonal throw pillows kind of wrecked the fairy tale thing. Hard to believe in forever when your childhood had a revolving door of 'meet your new dad'."

"That's a lot to carry," I said quietly.

She shrugged. "It just means I trust action more than words. Show me, don't promise me."

"I can respect that."

She tilted her head. "Your turn. What's your damage?"

I lifted my cup, buying a few seconds. "It's... complicated."

She arched a brow. "That's what people say when they want to sound deep without saying anything."

I chuckled. "Fair enough. I guess I grew up with a lot of expectations. Some of them were earned, some of them... not so much."

"Ah," she said, settling into her chair. "So, not chaotic line mine. More like... trying to fit into someone else's mold?"

"Exactly that." I glanced toward the trellis, where the breeze tugged at a stray napkin. "There was always this version of me people wanted me to be. I spent a long time trying to live up to it. Then I realized that wasn't how I wanted to live, so now I just do me."

She didn't respond right away. Just sipped her coffee and watched me like she was letting it all sink in.

Then she smiled faintly. "That explains the Hawaiian shirts."

I grinned. "It's a lifestyle choice."

"It's a *bold* choice."

"I stand by it."

"You would."

She traced the rim of her cup absently. Her bracelet caught the light—shells flashing pink and white like they had secrets.

"Today's been..." she started, then paused. "Unexpected."

"In a good way?"

Her eyes met mine. A beat passed. Two.

"Yeah," she said softly. "In a good way."

We let that hang there for a second. Warm. Open. Tipping toward something neither of us was ready to name.

Then she cleared her throat, sat up straighter, and smoothed her sundress like it could press the moment back into something safer.

"So, Mr. Hawaiian Shirt, do you have more island secrets? Or was that the grand finale?"

I stood and tossed my cup in the bin. "One more stop."

She raised a brow, clearly trying to look casual and failing. "Off the brochure?"

I smiled. "Of course! The best things always are."

Chapter Five

LOGAN

I TURNED OFF THE main path, ducking behind the shops and into the thick greenery at the edge of the resort. Piper followed without hesitation.

The trail narrowed, winding beneath a canopy of palms and tangled branches. We brushed them aside as we walked, the air heavy with humidity and birdsong. The scent of hibiscus and sea salt thickened with every step.

Then the trees parted—and we stepped into a secret.

Sunlight spilled over black volcanic rock and white sand. The grotto sparkled like it had been photoshopped, the water so clear and blue it looked enchanted.

Piper sucked in a breath. "OK. Wow."

"Most people don't come this way," I said. "You kind of have to know it's here."

"And you do because...?"

I shrugged, gaze drifting to the water. "Been around. Picked up a few secrets."

Not a lie. Just... edited.

She padded closer to the edge, eyes scanning the cove with that same sharp, curious look she'd given the kitchen knives earlier. Then, without a word, she crouched by a driftwood log, set down her phone and notebook, and slipped off her sandals.

Barefoot now, she crossed the sand toward the grotto

The sun hit her hair just right—a copper fire that glowed—and for a second, I forgot this was supposed to be a tour.

She moved toward the rock ledge that jutted over the water.

"Careful," I said, stepping forward. "That part gets slick."

She glanced over her shoulder, grinning. "What, no waiver?"

And then—she slipped.

Gone in a flash of limbs and spray.

"Piper!"

I didn't think. I jumped.

The water was colder than anything at the resort, sharp and clean. I plunged under, eyes open against the sting. For a second—just green-blue silence.

Then I saw her rising to the surface, not panicking or flailing.

Just... swimming.

I surfaced beside her, heart hammering. "Are you OK?"

She blinked at me, breathless but clearly fine. "Yeah. It's not exactly a cliff dive."

Her dress floated around her like seafoam. We treaded water, face-to-face, so close I saw droplets clinging to her lashes.

"You didn't have to jump in after me," she said, almost amused.

"Force of habit," I said, trying to keep it light. "Can't have the travel writer drowning on day one. Bad for Yelp."

She laughed, and it echoed across the rocks.

"I thought you were trying to be heroic."

"Yes, that. Is it working?" The words slipped out before I could stop them.

Her gaze met mine, and the world narrowed.

"Maybe a little," she said, voice soft.

One drop of water clung to her bottom lip, and I wanted to taste it so badly it hurt.

"We should probably get out," I said, not moving an inch.

"Probably," she echoed. Also not moving.

The water wrapped around us like a secret. Her leg brushed mine and heat reverberated through my body.

"You're staring," she whispered.

"Hard not to," I admitted.

She flushed, biting her lip. That droplet finally slid into the corner of her mouth, and I lost it.

"I should warn you," I murmured, "I'm about to do something extremely unprofessional."

A slow smile curved her lips. "That makes two of us."

I cradled her cheek, my fingers trailing water over her skin. "Last chance to stop me."

Instead, she fisted my shirt and pulled me in.

Our mouths met like a match to dry tinder—hot, fast, no hesitation. She tasted like salt and heat and something that might wreck me.

She pressed closer, arms wrapping around my neck, and I groaned into her mouth, deepening the kiss. The grotto disappeared. The world disappeared. It was just her—heat, lips, wet skin.

I moved us instinctively, kicking toward shallower water. She clung to me, legs around my waist, body warm and soft despite the chill. I reached the rock wall, steadying us with one hand while the other stayed tangled in her hair.

She pulled back just enough to whisper, breathless, "This wasn't in the resort brochure."

"Exclusive package," I murmured, tracing her lower lip with my thumb. "Limited availability."

Her smile turned wicked. "Do all your tours end like this?"

"Only the ones where the guest falls into a grotto."

She laughed, the sound vibrating against my chest.

Her dress clung to her now—wet and translucent, outlining every curve. Her legs squeezed tighter around my waist, and I felt her heat press against my cock.

"God, Piper," I groaned against her neck, pressing a kiss to the salt-slick skin.

She tilted her head, giving me more. "This is insane," she whispered. "This isn't... something I usually do."

"Me neither." And I meant it.

Her hands slid down my chest, exploring. When her thumbs brushed my nipples through my wet shirt, I nearly lost it.

PIPER

I couldn't believe this was happening.

Legs wrapped around a man I'd known for less than a day?—in a hidden grotto, kissing him like he held the answers to every question I'd never dared ask.

The rational part of my brain—the one trained on skepticism, deadlines, and investigative features—was protesting. This was unprofessional, reckless, and completely out of character.But for once, I didn't want to listen.

His hands were everywhere—skimming my thighs, tracing the curve of my waist, threading into my wet hair like he already knew how I liked to be touched. The cool water lapped around us, a delicious contrast to the heat coiling between our bodies.

"I want to touch you," I whispered against his lips, voice barely louder than the sound of the water. "Can I?"

Logan's eyes went dark, pupils wide with want. "Yes." Just one word, but it came out rough. Desperate.

I kept my legs hooked around him as my hand slipped beneath the surface. My fingers glided over the hard lines of his abs, twitching under my touch before drifting lower—finding the rigid outline of his cock through his shorts. The sharp inhale against my mouth made me feel suddenly powerful.

Even through the fabric, I could feel him pulse against my palm. I stroked him slowly, the water adding a dreamy drag to each motion.

"Fuck," he breathed, voice rasping against my neck. "That feels amazing."

Encouraged, I slipped my hand inside the waistband of his shorts. The moment I wrapped my fingers around his bare cock, we both gasped. He was smooth, hard, heavy in my grip, and the groan he let out had my pussy clenching around nothing.

"You're killing me," he growled, hips rocking into my palm as his fingers dug into my thighs, anchoring me to him.

I kept stroking him, drinking in the way his jaw clenched and his breath caught. Watching him unravel under my touch was more intoxicating than I ever expected.

"Tell me what you want," I whispered against his ear, surprising myself.

He didn't hesitate. His hands slid up under my dress, pushing it higher until they found the edge of my bikini bottoms. His fingers traced the seam—teasing, featherlight—before slipping beneath the damp fabric.

"I want to feel you," he said, his voice a low growl. "All of you."

I nodded, breath caught in my throat as his fingers found me—slick and aching despite the water around us.

"So wet," he murmured, circling my clit with maddening precision.

My grip on him faltered for a second as pleasure crashed through me, but I didn't stop. I couldn't. We were locked in some primal loop—me stroking him, him stroking me—neither of us willing to break the spell.

Logan slipped one finger inside me, then two, curling them just right. My hips jerked forward involuntarily, grinding against his hand as his thumb kept steady pressure on my clit.

"You feel incredible," he growled. "So damn tight."

I matched his pace, my strokes quickening, grip tightening around his cock. His hips bucked, and I felt him pulse against my palm again, close—so close.

The sight of his face—lips parted, eyes heavy, barely keeping it together—was almost enough to push me over the edge myself.

"Piper," he groaned, my name breaking from him like a plea. "I'm gonna come."

I twisted my wrist slightly, stroking faster. His rhythm between my legs faltered as he lost control. That, more than anything, undid me.

His head dropped to my shoulder, a deep, guttural moan tearing from his chest as he came in hot pulses into my hand. The sound echoed through the grotto like it had been waiting centuries to be heard.

He trembled against me, breath ragged, heart pounding.

He shifted us before I could catch my breath, lifting me like I weighed nothing and settling me on the smooth volcanic ledge. His eyes found mine—darker now, hungrier—and the air between us crackled.

"Your turn," he said, voice rough with promise.

And just like that, I was breathless all over again.

Chapter Six

LOGAN

I'D NEVER WANTED ANYTHING more in my life than I wanted to taste her right then.

Perched on the edge of the volcanic rock, thighs slightly parted, her wet dress clinging to every curve—she was pure fantasy. Water beaded down her legs, catching the sunlight like a trail of diamonds on her skin.

I hooked my fingers beneath the elastic of her bikini bottoms, dragging the fabric down her thighs slowly. She lifted her hips without a word—an invitation that made my pulse spike all over again. Even after everything, the hunger in me hadn't dulled. It had only sharpened.

The water lapped around my chest as I moved between her legs, tilting my head up to meet her eyes.

"You're beautiful," I murmured, kissing her thigh.

Her breath caught, fingers threading into my wet hair as I kissed higher and higher. She trembled under my touch, her grip tightening every time my mouth inched closer.

When I reached her pussy, I paused, looking up.

Her eyes—dark, wide, hungry—met mine. The raw need there nearly undid me.

"Please," she whispered, so soft it almost got lost in the lapping water.

I didn't make her repeat it.

I leaned in and ran my tongue over her wet pussy in one long, slow stroke. Her taste, an intoxicating mix of tangy and sweet, rocked me to my core. I knew I'd never get enough of that taste. She gasped, back arching, thighs tensing around my head.

"Oh God," she moaned, the sound echoing against the stone walls of the grotto.

I lost myself in her. Alternating between broad, greedy strokes and teasing circles around her clit, I couldn't get enough. I slipped my hands beneath her, lifting her slightly, angling her just right.

She gripped my hair tighter, her thighs trembling around my head as she writhed under my tongue. Each gasp, every moan that spilled from her lips lit me up like fire.

I slid two fingers inside her as my tongue kept working. She cried out, hips jerking, fingers curling hard in my hair.

"Logan," she gasped, and my name on her lips nearly broke me. "Don't stop. Please—don't stop."

As if I could.

I sucked gently, curling my fingers as I hit the spot that made her whole body jolt. Her moans turned frantic, hips moving against me, her voice dissolving into pleas.

"Yes, right there," she panted. "Just like that—"

I felt her start to come apart—tightening around my fingers, legs shaking, breath breaking into sharp little gasps. I looked up, needing to see her.

She was stunning—head thrown back, lips parted, copper hair wild and wet, like a jungle goddess in her element.

She came with my name on her lips, hips rolling, thighs clenching as waves of pleasure rippled through her. I felt it in my bones.

"Holy shit," she whispered, breathless, collapsing back against the warm rock.

We stayed like that for a moment. Her sprawled out, glowing and gorgeous. Me still in the water, catching my breath.

The grotto sounds returned—gentle water, birdsong, rustling palms. Her arm flopped over her eyes.

"Holy shit," she said again, and I couldn't help but smile as I pressed a soft kiss to her thigh before backing away.

"My thoughts exactly."

I helped her slide back into the water, her body loose and boneless against mine. She wrapped her arms around my neck, face tucked into my shoulder as we floated together.

I didn't want to move. Didn't want to let the real world creep in.

Her body felt perfect against mine as if we were built to fit this way. I traced lazy circles on her back as her breathing slowly evened out.

Her fingers traced lazy patterns on my chest, and even in the water, I couldn't hide my body's reaction. Despite having just found my own release minutes earlier, I was already hard again. The feel of her soft curves against me, the lingering taste of her on my tongue, the way she'd called my name when she came undone—it was intoxicating.

She must have felt it, because she shifted against me, her eyes meeting mine with a flash of surprise and unmistakable heat.

"Already?" she whispered, a smile playing at the corners of her mouth.

I laughed softly, feeling a mix of embarrassment and pride. "Apparently my body doesn't need a recovery period where you're concerned."

The water lapped gently around us as her arms tightened around my neck. Her pupils dilated, darkening those gorgeous green eyes. "I'm not complaining," she whispered, pressing a soft kiss to my jaw.

I groaned as her lips trailed up my neck. "As much as I want to continue this," I murmured against her ear, my hands sliding down to cup her ass beneath the water, "I don't have anything with me."

She pulled back slightly, eyes questioning.

"Protection," I clarified, brushing a wet strand of copper hair from her face.

The flicker of disappointment that crossed her face mirrored my own frustration. My body was screaming at me to keep going, to find a way, but the more rational part of my brain—the tiny sliver that could still think clearly with her pressed against me—knew better.

"We could head back to the resort," I suggested, my voice rough. "My suite has an impressive stock of... supplies."

Her eyes darkened, and she bit her lower lip—a small gesture that sent heat coursing through me.

"That sounds like an excellent idea," she whispered, her fingers trailing down my chest beneath the water.

I captured her hand before she could venture lower. "You keep that up, and we might not make it back," I warned, my voice a low growl.

She laughed, the sound bright and carefree in the secluded grotto. "Is that a challenge?"

I shook my head, smiling despite myself. "It's a promise."

I helped her up onto the warm stone ledge, water cascading down her curves as I followed. We wrung out our clothes as best we could, stealing glances and sharing secret smiles like teenagers sneaking around. Each accidental brush of skin against skin threatened to derail our plans to make it back to the resort.

"You're making this very hard," I murmured as she bent to pick up her sandals, giving me a view of her perfect ass.

She glanced over her shoulder, a mischievous smile playing on her lips. "That's the idea."

I groaned, adjusting myself in my shorts. "You're playing with fire, Piper."

"Good thing we're surrounded by water then," she quipped, straightening up and collecting her things.

She glanced over her shoulder, a mischievous smile playing on her lips. "That's the idea."

We made our way back through the lush foliage, hands intertwined, stopping every few feet to steal kisses that grew increasingly desperate. What should have been a fifteen-minute walk back to the resort took nearly twice as long.

By the time the white stone path of the resort grounds came into view, we were both breathless, my shorts uncomfortably tight, her eyes dark with want.

"My suite or yours?" I asked, thumb tracing circles on her palm.

"Yours," she replied without hesitation. "It's closer."

I led her through the resort's manicured gardens, nodding politely at a few passing resort staff who wisely kept their knowing smiles to themselves. My fingers tightened around hers as we approached the lobby.

PIPER

Just as we reached the lobby, a voice pulled me from the haze of the moment.

"There you are, Mr. Dawson," someone called from the check-in desk. "I have the revised itinerary from the regional team, and your four o'clock board call is confirmed."

I stopped walking.

Mr. Dawson.

The name snagged in my brain like a thread catching on something sharp.

Wait.

Dawson.

As in... Dawson Resorts?

My stomach dropped.

I turned to him slowly.

He'd gone still. Too still. The easy smile wiped clean off his face.

The woman handed him a folder, utterly unaware she'd just lit a match and tossed it onto a pile of kindling.

"You're Logan Dawson," I said, the words flat and cold on my tongue. "As in Logan Dawson the *CEO*?"

His mouth opened. "Piper, I was going to tell you—"

"When?" I asked, sharper than I meant to be, but I couldn't stop it. "After you got what you wanted? After I handed over all my notes and feedback like a helpful little idiot?"

His face fell. "That's not fair. It wasn't like that."

"Then what was it like, Logan?" I crossed my arms, acutely aware of my soaked dress, bare feet, and how ridiculous I must look. "Because from where I'm standing, it sure seems like you let me believe you were just some umbrella-adjusting pool guy."

"I never lied," he said, lowering his voice as a family with toddlers strolled past. "I just... didn't tell you everything."

I laughed. Not because it was funny. "Oh, great. Lies by omission. My favorite flavor of betrayal."

"I know how this looks," he said, stepping toward me.

I took one step back.

Something flickered across his face. Hurt. Or guilt. Maybe both.

"But I swear to you," he said, "what happened between us was real. I wasn't trying to get information out of you."

"Then why not introduce yourself like a normal human?" I asked, voice rising despite myself. "'Hi, I'm Logan Dawson, the guy whose empire you're here to write about.' Was that so hard?"

His hands dragged through his wet hair, flinging water droplets everywhere. "Because people change when they know. They either want something, get weirdly formal, or treat me like a walking ATM. I just... wanted to be me. With you."

"And what about what I wanted?" My voice cracked a little. "Did you even consider that maybe I deserved to know who I was dealing with?"

"You're not being fair," he said tightly. "I met you, and I liked you. Your passion, your honesty. The way you called me out without blinking? No one does that. Not in my world."

I stared at him. And God, some part of me wanted to believe him. Wanted it to be simple. Real.

But it wasn't.

"So, what was your endgame?" I asked, quieter now. "Let me leave thinking I'd had this whirlwind connection with some charming employee, only to realize later that I'd been fed a PR fantasy?"

"No, it wasn't like that," he looked away. "I didn't have a plan. I just... liked how it felt to be seen. Like a person."

That stopped me just for a breath.

Because I got it. I really did.

But that didn't make it okay.

"You should've told me," I said, softer now. The heat in my voice had cooled to something heavier. "You knew who I was. You knew why I was here."

"I didn't want to change how you looked at me."

"Well," I said, backing up another step, "mission failed."

I couldn't stay. Not here, not like this—wet, embarrassed, and furious with myself for feeling anything at all.

"I need to go," I muttered, wrapping my arms around myself despite the warm air.

"Piper—"

"Don't."

I turned before he could say anything else. Before he could explain, apologize, or make me want to stay.

And I walked away.

Each step felt heavier than the last—like I was dragging wet sand, salt, and the sting of disappointment along with me.

Chapter Seven

LOGAN

I watched her walk away.

Didn't chase her. Didn't call out.

Because seriously—what the hell was I supposed to say?

Hey, sorry I let you believe I was just some guy with a mild obsession with umbrellas and a thing for loud Hawaiian shirts? My bad for not disclosing that I own the resort you're writing an exposé about?

Yeah. That would go over great.

I stood there too long, dripping water onto the polished tile, ignoring the side-eyes from guests and the front desk staff who would turn this into a story before dinner service.

Eventually, I moved. No destination in mind—just *away*.

Somehow, I ended up in my suite, staring at the ocean like it owed me advice. Spoiler alert: it didn't.

I dried off. Changed. Paced. Considered texting her. Calling her. Writing something.

Did none of those.

Instead—God help me—I called Brett.

It rang twice before he answered. "Is the island on fire, or are you drunk-dialing me because you caught feelings?"

"Hi, Brett," I muttered, collapsing onto the couch. "Nice to hear your voice, too."

"OK, *now* I'm concerned. What did you do?"

"I didn't *do* anything," I said. Then sighed. "OK. I *may have* massively misjudged the situation."

Pause.

Then, "You didn't tell her who you were, did you?"

"Even worse. She found out before I could tell her. The front desk dropped the bomb."

Long pause.

Even Brett was stunned into silence.

Finally, he let out a low whistle. "So... the thing we both knew would blow up in your face? It blew up in your face."

"Spectacularly."

"She found out at the desk?"

"Yup. Right after the kind of moment that sears itself into your soul. Right after I started thinking maybe this wasn't just some vacation thing."

He exhaled, then gave a short laugh. "Man, you've really outdone yourself this time."

"I know," I muttered.

Brett sighed but his voice softened, the teasing fading a little. "You let her think you were someone else, Logan. That's... that's rough."

"I know," I repeated, rubbing my hand over my face. "I messed up."

A beat of silence.

"On the plus side," Brett said, trying to sound lighter, "You're officially in the 'emotionally tortured billionaire' club now. Welcome."

Then softer: "You going to let that be the end of it?"

I looked out at the ocean.

"No," I said. "Not even close."

I hung up and sat in silence, the echo of the grotto still burning into my brain—her laugh, her hands, the look in her eyes.

She deserved more than radio silence and regret.

I did the only thing that might matter. I went to her room

Not because I had any idea what to say, but because sometimes the best way forward is to go back to the beginning.

When I got there, I stood there, feeling like a damn fool. I knocked twice, not too soft, not too desperate.

Nothing.

I knocked again—louder.

The door swung open, and there she was. Hair damp, face clean, dressed in yoga pants and a loose tee that made her look ten times more devastating than she had earlier. Her eyes widened when she saw me, then narrowed.

"If you're here to explain—"

"I'm not," I said, holding up my hands in a gesture of surrender. "I just... needed to apologize. For everything. For keeping the truth from you."

She stared at me for a long moment, arms crossed, her hair beginning to curl around her face as it dried.

"I'm sorry you found out the way you did," I said after she didn't speak. "I should have told you from the beginning."

She laughed, but there was no humor in it. "Yeah, that would have been the decent thing to do."

"I should've told you," I repeated quietly. "I just... got caught up in something, something I wasn't ready to lose."

My eyes searched for any sign that she might understand, might believe me. "I didn't want to lose the way you saw me. But that was selfish. And cowardly. I get that now."

She was quiet for a long beat, her expression unreadable.

"What exactly did you think was going to happen, Logan?" she finally said, my name sounding different on her lips now that she knew the weight it carried. "That we'd have some vacation fling and then you'd what—wave goodbye as I wrote my article about your resort without ever knowing who you really were?"

I winced. When she put it that way, it sounded even worse.

"I didn't think that far ahead," I admitted. "I just... liked being someone who wasn't defined by his net worth for once."

Her eyes flashed. "So I was an experiment in normalcy?"

"No. God, no." I ran a hand through my still-damp hair. "You were—are—the most real thing I've felt in years."

"You know what I keep thinking about?" she finally said, her voice quieter than I expected. "Every time you smiled at me or made some stupid joke about umbrellas or told me about the gecko or the koi—was any of that real? Or was it just some game to you? The billionaire slumming it with the reporter?"

The accusation stung, but I deserved it.

"All of it was real," I said, the words rushing out before I could overthink them. "That's the problem. I've never been more myself than I was with you. The title, the money, the reputation—none of that matters when I'm with you. For the first time in years, I was just... Logan."

Piper's eyes widened slightly, and I could see her fighting against wanting to believe me. Her shoulders stayed rigid, but something in her expression softened.

"That's the thing, Logan," she said, my name still sounding foreign on her lips. "I don't know who 'just Logan' is anymore. The man I thought I was getting to know doesn't exist."

"He does," I insisted, taking half a step forward before stopping myself. "The umbrella guy? The one who knows the names of all fish? The one who nearly drowned showing off for you? That's me. The only difference is that I sign the paychecks."

She leaned against the doorframe, not inviting me in but not slamming the door in my face either. Progress.

"And what about my article?" she asked.

Chapter Eight

PIPER

I KNEW I SHOULD slam the door in his face. It was the logical move—the self-respecting one. But I could still feel the phantom touch of his hands on my me in the grotto, how he made me feel powerful and beautiful all in one. I could still hear the echo of his moan bouncing off the stone walls.

And looking at him standing there, hair still damp, his eyes holding a vulnerability I hadn't seen before... it complicated things. Damn him.

"What about my article?" I repeated when he didn't immediately answer. "Was this all some elaborate scheme to manipulate what I write?"

"No," he said firmly. "The article was never the point."

"Then what was the point, Logan?" I crossed my arms tighter. "Because from where I'm standing, you've been playing me since the umbrella incident."

"Your article is your article," he said, his voice steady despite the weariness in his eyes. "I'm not asking you to change a word of what you write. That's not why I'm here."

"Then why are you here?" I pressed, trying to keep my voice from betraying how conflicted I felt. Part of me wanted to tell him to leave, that it was too late. The other part—the stupid, foolish part—wanted to let him in, to hear him out.

He exhaled slowly. "Because I couldn't let things end like that. Not without telling you that everything between us was real. The only lie was what I left out—the fact that I'm the CEO."

I wanted to believe him. That was the terrifying part—how much I wanted those words to be true. How much I wanted his deception to be a simple omission rather than a calculated move.

"That's still a pretty big thing not to say," I replied, my voice softer than I intended. "You're not just some guy who works here, Logan. You're literally the man behind the curtain."

He ran a hand through his hair, making it stand up in places. It made him look younger, less polished. More like the Logan I thought I knew.

"I know," he said. "And I know it changes things. But I'm asking—begging, really—for a chance. Just a chance."

I twisted the shell bracelet on my wrist, hearing the older woman's voice in my head. *Real love doesn't question. It recognizes.*

"I can't be objective about this place anymore," I admitted. "Not after today. Not after... you."

Logan was quiet for a moment, eyes on the bracelet. "What if you don't have to be?"

I looked up. "What?"

"Write what actually happened," he said. "The good and the bad. How you felt being here—as a traveler, not as a journalist."

"That's not how this works," I said automatically. But even I could hear the hesitation in my voice. "It's supposed to be unbiased."

"Isn't it more honest to admit when something affects you?" he asked. "Isn't *that* transparency?"

I bit my lip. He had a point. One that made me uncomfortable because it poked at something I hadn't wanted to examine too closely—how much of my job had become performative instead of an authentic experience.

"I don't think my editor would go for that."

"Have you ever asked?"

No. I hadn't. I'd been so busy trying to prove I couldn't be bought I'd stopped allowing myself to *feel*.

"No," I admitted.

"I'm not asking you to lie," he said, voice low. "Or even be kind. Just... be honest. About *everything*."

"Including the CEO who pretended to be staff?"

"If it's relevant, write it," he said with a faint smile. "Though maybe skip the grotto chapter. For both our reputations."

A laugh escaped me before I could stop it. "Yeah, I think I'll leave that part out."

Our eyes locked. And just like that, the tension softened into something else. Something charged.

"For what it's worth," he said, "today was the most real I've felt in a long time. Not because I was pretending. But because, for once, I *wasn't*."

I wanted to believe him. And staring into those eyes, I *did*. There was no agenda in them. Just sincerity.

"One hundred percent yourself, huh?" I asked. "Including the part where you fell off a paddleboard trying to impress me?"

He laughed, and the sound warmed something inside me. "Especially that part. Old me would've had the staff rig those boards to prevent CEO embarrassment."

"That actually tracks."

His smile was genuine, a little uncertain. For a man who owned a luxury resort empire, he looked surprisingly vulnerable.

I stepped back, opening the door wider. "Do you want to come in? Just to talk," I added quickly. "I think we have a lot to figure out."

LOGAN

I hesitated at the threshold, weighing the implications of stepping into her room. This felt significant—like crossing a boundary we couldn't uncross.

"You sure?" I asked, giving her a chance to reconsider.

She nodded, stepping aside. "Just talking."

"Just talking," I agreed, moving past her into the suite.

The room smelled like her—that hint of perfume and something uniquely Piper. Her laptop sat open on the desk beside scattered notes. A half-empty glass of wine stood on the nightstand. The bed was rumpled, as if she'd been sitting on it before I knocked.

It was disarmingly intimate, seeing her space like this.

"Nice view," I said, nodding toward the balcony where the ocean stretched endlessly.

"It is," she agreed, closing the door behind me. "Though I'm guessing yours is better."

I laughed. "My view's actually worse. North wing faces the gardens."

"Seriously?" She looked genuinely surprised. "Why wouldn't you give yourself the best view?"

I shrugged, feeling oddly self-conscious. "Best views go to the paying guests. It's just business. But I like the gardens. They're... quieter. The ocean is beautiful, but sometimes it feels like it's shouting at you to appreciate it."

Piper tilted her head, studying me with new interest. "That's... unexpectedly poetic."

"Don't sound so surprised." I smiled, leaning against the wall beside the doors. "There's a lot you don't know about me."

"That's becoming increasingly obvious." She sat on the edge of the bed, tucking one leg underneath her. "So tell me something real. Something I wouldn't know from your LinkedIn profile."

I laughed, settling into a chair. "That's a loaded question."

I thought for a moment, wanting to give her something genuine. Not the rehearsed soundbites I trotted out for investors or the carefully curated personal details I shared in interviews.

"I hate flying," I finally said. "Everyone assumes with the private jets and island-hopping that I must love it, but I white-knuckle it every time."

Piper's eyebrows shot up. "You're kidding. But you own resorts all over the world."

"I know. Ironic, right?" I ran a hand through my hair. "I've tried everything—meditation, therapy, even hypnosis once. Nothing works. I just grip the armrests and pretend I'm not terrified until we land."

Piper's smile was soft, unexpectedly tender. "That's... oddly reassuring."

"That I'm a mess when I fly?"

"That there's something the great Logan Dawson isn't good at." She tucked a strand of hair behind her ear. "Makes you seem more human."

"Oh, there's a long list of things I'm terrible at," I said, relaxing a bit. "I can't make a decent outfit to save my life. I have no idea what to do with a tie, and if you ask me to match colors, you're better off letting a toddler pick out your clothes."

Piper chuckled, clearly amused. "The CEO of a global resort chain can't even match his clothes?"

"Yeah, it's a little embarrassing," I admitted. "I leave that up to the experts. Most of the time, I just wear Hawaiian shirts and pretend I know what I'm doing."

Piper laughed outright, shaking her head. "Well, you certainly pull it off better than most."

"That's because I know when to let the shirt have its moment," I said with a grin. "It's all about confidence."

"Confidence, huh?" She raised an eyebrow, clearly not buying it.

"Okay, maybe not all of it," I said, leaning back in my chair. "But it works for me."

Piper reached for her wine glass, taking a sip as she studied me. "So, Hawaiian shirts and fear of flying. What else should I know about the real Logan Dawson?"

I shifted in my seat, considering. "I haven't taken a real vacation in five years. The kind where you actually disconnect. Every 'vacation' has been work in disguise."

"That's... sad," she said, her voice softening.

"Is it?" I shrugged. "I love what I do. I built this company from nothing. It's hard to step away."

"But at what cost?" She set her glass down. "When was the last time you did something just because it made you happy? Not because it was good for business or part of some master plan?"

I opened my mouth to answer, then closed it again. The truth was, I couldn't remember. Every decision, every action for years had been calculated, weighed against how it would affect the business.

Except for the day with her.

"This," I finally said. "Being with you. That's the first thing I've done in years that wasn't about the bottom line."

Her eyes widened slightly, and I could see the conflict there—wanting to believe me, but still wary.

"Is that why you didn't tell me who you were? Because you wanted to hold onto that feeling?" she asked softly.

I leaned forward, resting my elbows on my knees. "Partly. When you didn't know who I was, you treated me like... just a guy. Not a portfolio or a business opportunity. Do you have any idea how rare that is?"

Her expression softened. "I guess I never thought about it that way."

"Most people don't," I said, trying not to sound bitter. "When you have money, everyone wants something. A job, an investment, a connection. It gets exhausting wondering if people like you or just what you can do for them."

"So you lied to me because you assumed I'd be like everyone else?" There was a hint of hurt in her voice.

"No," I said quickly. "I didn't tell you because I liked how it felt to just be me. The guy with the umbrella obsession. Not Logan Dawson, CEO. And then it got complicated."

I ran my hand through my hair, trying to find the right words.

"I didn't plan any of this, Piper. I was just going to check out that stupid umbrella situation, and then... there you were. And I couldn't walk away."

She studied me, her eyes searching mine. "But you must have known it would come out eventually. This is a small island."

"I did," I admitted. "I just... kept pushing it off. Telling myself I'd figure it out later."

"That doesn't sound like the strategic businessman I've read about."

I laughed softly. "Yeah, well, turns out I make terrible decisions when I'm falling for someone."

The words hung in the air between us. I hadn't meant to say that part out loud.

Piper's breath caught. The air between us charged with electricity, making the small space feel even more intimate.

"Falling for someone?" she echoed, her voice barely above a whisper.

I could've backtracked. Could've laughed it off as a figure of speech. But I was done pretending.

"Yeah," I said, meeting her gaze steadily. "That would be you."

She looked down at her hands, twisting that shell bracelet again. When she looked up, her eyes held a mixture of caution and hope that made my heart stutter.

"This is crazy," she murmured. "You're... you. And I'm supposed to be writing an objective piece about your resort."

"Yep," I said. "But here we are."

"Here we are," she echoed, her voice soft.

I didn't want to push, so I waited, letting the silence settle between us. The ball was in her court now.

Finally, she looked up, a small smile playing at her lips. "I should probably be more upset with you," she said. "But the problem is... I think I'm falling for you too. The real you—the umbrella guy, terrible fashion choices and all."

My heart hammered in my chest. "Yeah?"

"Yeah." She tucked a strand of hair behind her ear, her nervous habit.

I let out a breath, the weight of her words hitting me harder than I expected. "I don't have a playbook for this," I admitted. "I'm not sure what happens next."

"That makes two of us." She chuckled softly, the sound warm. "I've never had a billionaire CEO hide his identity from me before."

"And I've never had a travel journalist see through all my walls." I smiled, something light sparking inside me. "Guess we're both in uncharted territory."

Piper stood up and walked toward the sliding glass door, opening it to let in the ocean breeze. The sound of the waves rolling against the shore made the quiet between us feel even more charged.

She turned to face me, her eyes soft but intense. "We could start over," she said, the breeze playing with her hair. "Or we could just... continue. Pick up where we left off, but with all our cards on the table this time."

I stepped toward her, drawn in. Standing beside her, close but not touching, I whispered, "I'd like that. Continuing."

She gave a slow nod, her expression turning serious. "But you need to understand something, Logan," she said, her gaze steady. "I won't compromise my integrity. Whatever I write about Coral Bay, it'll be honest."

"I wouldn't expect anything less," I said, meaning it. "Your honesty is one of the things I admire most about you."

For a long moment, we stood there, the sea breeze swirling around us, and I realized that no matter what came next, this was worth fighting for.

Epilogue

LOGAN

Six months later...

I'd heard the front door before I saw her.

The soft thud of her suitcase hitting the hardwood. The rustle of fabric. The quiet sigh she always let out the second she got home from a trip.

My chest squeezed.

Three weeks without her had been too damn long.

I stepped out of the kitchen, drying my hands on a towel, just as Piper dropped her carry-on and looked up. Hair tousled. Sun-kissed skin and tired eyes that lit up the second they landed on me.

She smiled—and just like that, everything inside me settled.

"There you are," I said, crossing the space between us.

"You didn't have to wait up," she murmured, even as she wrapped her arms around my waist and melted into me.

"I always wait up."

She smelled like salt, sunshine, and faint airport coffee, and I didn't care. I buried my face in her hair and held her like I planned to do for the rest of my life.

"Miss me?" she mumbled against my chest.

"Every. Damn. Day."

She laughed softly, tilting her face up. "Even when I kept sending you photos of sketchy hotel buffets and that guy with the lizard on his shoulder?"

"Especially then." I kissed her—slow and deep. The kind of kiss you save for homecomings. "Welcome back."

We stood there for a long moment, just breathing each other in.

"I should probably shower," she murmured against my lips. "Airplane and all that."

"Mmm." I agreed but made no effort to let her go. Instead, I kissed her again, hands sliding down to her hips, pulling her closer. Three weeks without her had been torture. Every video call had only made me miss her more.

"Logan," she laughed, pushing gently against my chest. "I'm serious. I smell like recycled air and that weird sandwich they served on the flight."

"Don't care," I muttered, pressing my lips to her neck.

She shivered, her hands finding their way into my hair. "You will when I'm in your clean sheets."

"Our sheets," I corrected, reluctantly pulling back to look at her.

"Our sheets," she conceded, giving me that little smile I'd missed every night for twenty-one days. She stepped back, linking her fingers with mine. "So... about that shower."

I knew that tone. It was the one that made my pulse quicken, and my thoughts scatter.

"Need help scrubbing your back?" I asked, aiming for casual and missing by a mile.

She tugged me toward the bathroom, her exhaustion seemingly forgotten. "Among other things."

I followed like a man possessed, watching as she dropped her jacket on the hallway floor and kicked off her shoes at the bathroom door. By the time we reached the master bath, she was already pulling her shirt over her head, revealing the expanse of sun-kissed skin I'd been dreaming about.

I reached past her to turn on the shower, setting it to the temperature she liked—hot enough to steam the mirrors but not scald. The thick fog began to fill the space as Piper stepped out of her jeans, revealing a simple black thong that made my mouth go dry.

"You going to just stand there and watch?" she asked, a playful challenge in her eyes.

I shook my head, unbuttoning my shirt with fingers that suddenly felt clumsy. "Just enjoying the view."

She reached behind her back to unhook her bra, letting it fall to the tile. After three weeks apart, the sight of her—all of her hit me like a physical force. My body responded instantly, every nerve ending alive and electric.

"God, I've missed you," I breathed, stepping closer.

She helped me with my belt, her fingers brushing against me in a way that couldn't possibly be accidental. "Show me how much."

I didn't need to be told twice.

We stepped into the shower together, and the world narrowed to just us. Just this. Her naked body gleamed under the water, her copper hair darkening as it got wet, clinging to her shoulders like she was some kind of water goddess.

"God, I've missed touching you," I murmured against her neck, tasting the water droplets gathering there. "Three weeks is too damn long."

Piper arched into me, her fingers digging into my shoulders. "I know. The last hotel had this pathetic excuse for a shower."

I pressed her back against the cool tile as the water cascaded over us. Her skin was slick beneath my hands, and I couldn't stop touching her—memorizing her all over again like it was the first time.

"Every night," I confessed, my voice rough with want, "I'd lie in our bed thinking about this. About you."

Her eyes darkened, pupils dilating as she wrapped one leg around my hip, pulling me closer. The feel of her—soft and warm and wet—was almost too much.

"Show me," she whispered, and it wasn't a request.

I lifted her, both hands cupping her ass as she wrapped her legs around my waist. The water pounded against my back as I pressed her into the tile wall, my mouth finding hers in a kiss that was all hunger and heat.

She moaned into my mouth, her fingers tangling in my wet hair, tugging in that way she *knew* drove me wild. I growled against her lips, grinding my cock against her.

"Logan," she gasped, breaking the kiss. "I need you. Now."

I shifted her slightly, positioning myself at her entrance. "Tell me again, was there something you wanted?"

"If you don't fuck me right now," she interrupted, eyes blazing with desire, "I might actually die."

I couldn't help but laugh—even now, she was still my Piper. Direct. Demanding and perfect.

With one smooth thrust, I buried myself inside her.

"Fuck," I groaned, my forehead resting against hers as I fought for control. "You feel incredible."

She whimpered, her inner walls clenching around me as she adjusted to the fullness. "Don't stop," she breathed against my ear. "Please don't stop."

I began to move, finding a rhythm that had her gasping with each thrust. The shower spray created a cocoon around us, the steam rising as our bodies moved together. Water cascaded down her breasts, and I couldn't resist leaning forward to capture one peaked nipple between my lips.

"Yes," she moaned, her head falling back against the tile. "God, I've thought about this every night."

I shifted my angle slightly, hitting that spot inside her that made her cry out. "Tell me," I said softly, never breaking my rhythm. "Tell me what you thought about."

Her eyes fluttered open, dark with desire. "You. Inside me. Making me come so hard I forget my own name."

That was all I needed to hear.

I increased my pace, my grip tightening on her thighs as I drove deeper. The water ran in rivulets between our bodies, adding another layer of sensation to every thrust, every touch. Her nails dug into my shoulders, the slight sting only heightening my pleasure.

"Look at me," I growled, my voice barely recognizable. "I want to see you when you come."

Her eyes locked with mine, vulnerable and trusting and blazing with need. The connection between us transcended the physical—it always had, from that first day by the palm tree.

"I'm close," she gasped, her body beginning to tremble. "So close—"

I slid one hand between us, finding her swollen clit with my thumb. One gentle circle and she cried out, her inner walls clenching around me like a vice, her whole body shaking with release.

"Logan!" she cried, the sound echoing off the tile as she shattered.

The sight of her coming undone—head thrown back, eyes locked on mine, lips parted in ecstasy—pushed me over the edge. I thrust once, twice more before burying myself deep inside her, my own orgasm tearing through me.

"Piper," I groaned her name a prayer as I pulsed inside her.

For several long moments, we stayed like that—connected, breathing hard, the water raining down on us in a steady rhythm. Her legs remained wrapped around my waist, our foreheads pressed together.

"I love you," I whispered, the words simple, true.

Her fingers traced my jawline, her gaze warm and sure. "I love you too. So much."

I carefully lowered her, steadying her as her feet touched the tile. Her legs trembled slightly, and I couldn't help but smile.

"Welcome home," I murmured against her temple.

"Mmm, quite the homecoming," she said with a lazy smile, reaching for the shampoo. "Though I should probably actually get clean now."

We washed off in companionable silence—the kind that only exists between people who've learned each other's rhythms. We got out and I handed her a towel—one of the oversized fluffy ones she insisted on buying when she moved in—and grabbed one for myself.

She wrapped herself in the towel, tucking it securely above her breasts, while I slung mine low on my hips. Her wet hair hung in dark copper waves down her back, and I couldn't resist running my fingers through it, separating the strands. She leaned into my touch like a cat, eyes closing briefly with contentment.

"You hungry?" I asked, pressing a kiss to her shoulder. "I made that pasta thing you like."

Her head tilted up instantly. "The one with the crispy prosciutto?"

I nodded, trying not to look too pleased with myself.

Her eyes lit up. "God, you're perfect."

"I try," I said, grinning as I grabbed a towel and gently started drying her damp hair. "Let me—"

The shrill ring of my phone cut through the moment.

I groaned, already recognizing the custom ringtone.

"Brett," I muttered.

Piper chuckled and leaned back. "Go ahead. I'll pretend I'm not picturing you in an apron right now."

I swiped to answer and pressed the phone to my ear. "This better be important," I said as a greeting.

Brett's voice came through loud and exasperated. "Liz is breathing down my neck. Says her best friend Mia is about to spontaneously combust and needs a break from life before she breaks her espresso machine—or someone's kneecaps."

I shot Piper a look. "So you're calling me for a favor?"

"She needs a vacation. Somewhere far away. With fruity drinks and no Wi-Fi," Brett said. "She's like a human firecracker with a design genius brain and zero filter."

I glanced toward the kitchen, where dinner was waiting. "Send me her info. I'll make sure she gets the VIP treatment. Maybe the beach will mellow her out."

"Doubtful," Brett replied. "But it'll make Liz stop threatening to design a voodoo doll with my face on it."

"Mia, huh?" I said, mostly to myself, as I hung up the phone, a grin pulling at my mouth. "Hope the island's ready."

Unraveling Mr. Ashford

A Flirty, Spicy Romcom with a Grumpy Tech Billionaire, a Sunshine Chaos Bomb, and a Storm That Changed Everything

Hana York

Pink Pop Publishing

Unraveling Mr. Ashford

(Don't Fall for the Billionaire Book 3)

Copyright © 2025 by Hana York

www.HanaYork.com

Contents

Chapter One

MIA

I was about to land in paradise—and if I kept grinning like the Chesire Cat, I might actually prove my mom right: my face *could* get stuck that way. But who cared? After the Great Vision Board Inferno of last week—yes, it *literally* caught fire—I'd taken it as a sign. I was overdue for a break.

So I called Liz. Who called Brett. Who called Logan.

And now? I was on a boat headed to a private island, courtesy of the world's most well-connected favor chain. Just me, Mia Wilder—overcaffeinated chaos goddess—on my way to a man-made oasis where the only thing on my agenda was doing absolutely nothing.

"Alright, universe," I said, arms wide to the sea breeze, "hit me with your best vacation vibes. I'm ready."

The boatman glanced at me like he was debating whether to offer a lifejacket for enthusiasm-induced overboard risks. But I didn't care. This was my time. No deadlines. No emails. Just me, the ocean, and whatever cocktail came with a paper umbrella and questionable fruit garnish.

As we neared the island, the tension I hadn't even realized I was holding began to unravel. Each tiny island had its own bungalow, tucked into palm trees like something off a movie poster. Quiet. Secluded. Bliss.

The second we bumped the dock, I was on my feet—bag slung over one shoulder, hat in hand, ready to disembark.

"Thanks for the ride!" I called as I stepped onto the dock, giving the boatman a wave he didn't return. Rude. But whatever. I was unreachable now. Possibly glowing. Definitely smug.

I paused for a slow, dramatic spin. Theme music: internal. Vibe: tropical main character energy.

The bungalow sat nestled between swaying palms and completely unfair postcard-level views. There was even a hammock. A *hammock*. I had arrived.

The air smelled like sea salt, warm breeze, and pure freedom. I followed the winding stone path up to the front door, trailing my fingers across the fronds like I was starring in a spa commercial. No people. No notifications. No inbox from hell. Just me and whatever was waiting inside.

The door swung open into a space that was bright, breezy, and gave off serious *rich people Pinterest board* energy. Fruit on the counter. Towels rolled with spiritual intent. A bar cart.

It was perfect.

"This is it," I whispered, pausing in the doorway like I was about to marry the space. "We're in love. I live here now. Someone forward my mail."

I tossed my bag onto the couch with dramatic flair—because if you weren't making a grand entrance for an audience of throw pillows, were you even vacationing properly?

Step one: unpack essentials. Sunglasses. SPF 50. Journal. Three pens. Emergency chocolate. Backup emergency chocolate. Sketchbook I swore I wouldn't touch. Not even once.

I stared at it for a beat, the blank cover practically whispering *you know you want to.* "Nope," I muttered, tossing it face-down on the coffee table like it couldn't seduce me if I avoided eye contact. "You are not the boss of me."

Next stop: the bedroom.

It had a four-poster bed draped in gauzy white curtains and approximately fifty-seven pillows. The kind of setup that whispered *you are adored, and your spine will be perfectly aligned by morning.* I flopped onto the mattress with a happy sigh and immediately did a snow angel—luxury linen edition.

"This is fine," I told the ceiling. "This is totally normal."

Back in the main room, I cracked open the mini-fridge and gasped. Sparkling water. Fresh juice. Chocolate-covered almonds. And one of those tiny glass bottles of milk like you'd find at a farmer's market curated by influencers with goats.

Juice in hand, I stepped outside.

The deck had a private plunge pool and two lounge chairs angled like they were in a competition for best ocean view. I sank into one like a queen returning to her throne—juice in one hand, sunglasses perched like a crown, hair already frizzing in joyful rebellion. Whatever. I was relaxed. I was glowing. I was *totally* not wondering if my sketchbook missed me.

I closed my eyes and soaked it in—the breeze, the waves, the beautiful absence of anyone needing anything from me.

This was the right choice.

Definitely the right—

CRACK.

My eyes flew open.

Was that thunder?

I glanced at the horizon.

The sky, which had been a soft watercolor of vacation bliss, now had a dramatic smear of gray creeping in from the edge. One cloud. Maybe two. But definitely not enough to panic over.

"Do not ruin this for me," I whispered at the ocean, pointing my juice like a tiny, citrus-scented threat.

GRANT

The boat rocked harder than expected as we crossed the last stretch of open water. I stayed seated, jaw tight, one hand gripping the edge of the bench—not because I was nervous. Just tired. The kind of tired that sleep didn't fix. The kind you carried in your bones after too many meetings, too many "urgent" emails, too many people who saw a title, not a person.

The boatman glanced back. "You sure about this? Storm's rolling in faster than expected."

I exhaled through my nose. "I'll be fine."

He checked again a minute later. "If it hits hard, you might lose signal for a while."

"Perfect," I muttered. "I didn't come to talk to anyone."

He gave me a look—half annoyed, half curious—but left it alone.

Good. I wasn't here to explain myself. I came to disappear. To shut the world out for a while. If a little weather helped keep it at bay? Even better.

By the time we reached the dock, the clouds had thickened, the sky gone from pale blue to a heavy slate gray. Wind pushed against the hull, rough enough to knock the boat harder than it should've against the dock.

I slung my duffel over my shoulder and stepped off without waiting for help.

"Last chance," the boatman said, still eyeing the horizon. "Sure you don't want to ride it out at the main resort?"

"This is the plan," I said. "I'll be fine."

He didn't argue. Just nodded and shifted into reverse. Within seconds, the hum of the engine was swallowed by wind and waves.

I stood there a beat longer, watching him disappear. The bungalow sat tucked between the palms, quiet and pristine. Everything I'd asked for.

Everything I needed.

I just hoped the storm—whatever kind it turned out to be—held off long enough to let me breathe.

The path to the bungalow wound through swaying trees, damp fronds brushing my shoulders, the scent of rain already in the air. A few coconuts dotted the trail like nature's speed bumps. The wind picked up, first drops of rain tapping the roof as I stepped onto the porch.

From the outside, it looked exactly like I'd hoped.

Quiet. Still.

Then I opened the door—and flinched.

Music.

Loud, bright, aggressively cheerful music blasted through the space like it was prepping for a bachelorette weekend. And there—spinning barefoot in the center of the room—was a woman.

Pink bikini top. Sarong slipping off one hip. Hair wild and curly, bouncing with every step. Lips moving along with the lyrics like she was the star of her own music video. Effortless. Radiant.

Beautiful.

The kind of beautiful that made you pause. That made it hard not to notice the smooth legs, the swing of her hips, the soft glow of her skin.

And my body—utter traitor—noticed all of it.

I told myself to look away.

I didn't.

Instead, I stood there. Stunned. Irritated. A little alarmed at how fast my brain forgot why I came here in the first place.

This was not part of the plan.

I came for silence.

Not a barefoot sun goddess twirling through my sanctuary like she *was* the weather.

I cleared my throat.

Loudly.

She didn't hear me.

Of course she didn't.

So I stepped fully inside, letting the door slam shut behind me.

She shrieked and skidded to a stop, nearly slipping on her own sarong, eyes going wide like I'd materialized out of thin air.

"WHAT THE ACTUAL HELL—WHO ARE YOU?! Are you lost? Are you a serial killer? Because I've got to tell you, *today is not the day!*"

"I could ask you the same thing," I said, deadpan. "This is supposed to be *my* bungalow."

And just like that, peace was officially off the itinerary.

Chapter Two

MIA

He was grumpy.

And tall.

And did I mention grumpy?

What in the brooding, broad-shouldered lumberjack fantasy had just walked through my door?

I blinked, still holding my juice like a weapon, trying to process the fact that the human embodiment of a moody Greek god was standing in my sacred, self-care sanctuary looking like I'd personally offended him by existing.

"This is supposed to be your bungalow?" I repeated, breathless. "Oh no. Nope. Absolutely not."

He didn't answer—just stood there, jaw tight, arms crossed, silently judging me and possibly all spontaneous dance breaks.

But his eyes were kind. Unfairly so. The kind that said he'd help old ladies cross the street without waiting for thanks. And those shoulders? They could absolutely carry a roof beam. Or me. Through a flood. Probably shirtless.

Focus, Mia.

"Yes, my bungalow," he said, dragging a hand through his hair like I'd just asked him to solve a Rubik's cube in the dark. "Booked through the week."

"You're joking."

He was not joking. He looked like he didn't know how to joke.

Muscles. Mood. Mystery. And now: a walking, talking cancellation of my spa-vibes-only vacation plan.

This was supposed to be *my* week. Hammocks. Face masks. Utter, uninterrupted bliss.

Not... this.

Definitely not *him*.

I grabbed the phone and stabbed in the resort number like I was starting a duel. "We'll see about this, Mr. Tall-Dark-and-Uninvited," I muttered. "You may be hot, but you're also extremely grumpy, which cancels out, like, sixty percent of the appeal."

A low voice behind me: "Did you just call me hot?"

I jumped. "No. I mean—yes. But not in a *come hither* way. More like an observational data point. Like 'the sky is blue' or 'fruit should not be room temperature'."

He just stared at me. Unmoved. Like I'd said I was building a shrine to throw pillows and anxiety.

"And anyway," I added, flailing for dignity, "it doesn't count if you're *that* grumpy."

Still nothing.

Tall. Judgy. Unbothered. Gorgeous.

"Okay, seriously," I muttered, turning away. "Stop looking at me like that. I'm flustered, not unhinged. Just... unhinged-adjacent."

The line picked up. A cheerful voice chirped, "Hi, Isla Cove Resort—how can I—"

"Yes! Hi! " I said, too loud and too fast. "There's been a mistake. I'm on Island Seven, and there's a man here. Like, a full-grown *grumpy* man. Not a staff member. Not a hallucination. Real. Broody. Cheekbones that could start wars—anyway, not important."

Grant crossed his arms tighter. Statue mode: activated.

"I was told this bungalow was mine for the week," I pressed on. "But apparently Mr. 'Resting Glare Face' got the same memo. So if someone could just—"

Crack.

A pop. Then static. Then nothing.

I stared at the phone. "No, no, no. Don't you die on me now, signal bar. You were my last hope."

Dead. Gone. Zero bars.

I lifted the phone like a peace offering to the sky. "Come on," I hissed. "Not when I've just declared war on a man who bench-presses silence for sport."

The man didn't say a word. But I felt his stare.

I turned my back to him and moved toward the window, waving the phone like I was summoning a miracle. No signal. No help. No justice.

"Okay," I whispered. "Not panicking. This is fine. I'm not stranded on a private island with a hot stranger who thinks I'm in *his* bungalow."

And then—because of course—the skies opened up.

Buckets of rain. Wind howling. Palms bent sideways. A pair of flip-flops launched off the porch like they were trying to escape the narrative.

When I turned around, *he* was still standing there. Annoyed. A little smug.

"Looks like we're both stuck," I said flatly.

GRANT

The rain slammed against the roof like it had a vendetta.

I pulled out my phone, already knowing what I'd see. One bar. Then none.

"No signal," I muttered.

Across the room, the woman I was apparently stranded with let out a dramatic sigh and dropped onto the couch like the storm had personally betrayed her.

"Spectacular," she muttered. "Just absolutely peak timing. Stuck on an island with Mr. Corporate Brood and zero internet. This is fine. Totally fine. Like, aggressively fine."

I didn't respond.

Partly because I didn't trust myself not to laugh. Mostly because I still wasn't convinced this wasn't some kind of cosmic prank.

She waved her juice glass toward me without looking. "Okay. Since we're doing this, I need to vet you."

"Vet me?"

"Yes. I've seen this movie. Guy shows up during a storm, no one can verify his identity, and boom—surprise murder."

"I'm not a murderer," I said flatly.

She squinted. "That's exactly what a murderer would say."

I exhaled slowly. "What do you want to know?"

"Name. Job. Zodiac sign. Go."

I gave her a look, but she just raised her brows like she was taking attendance.

"Grant Ashford. CEO. Virgo."

Her eyes narrowed slightly. "Virgo. Yeah, that explains the vibe."

I had no idea what that meant, and I wasn't about to ask.

She leaned forward, studying me like a case study. "CEO of what?"

"Tech. Infrastructure. Startups. Boring stuff."

She whistled. "So you're rich-rich."

"I'm tired-tired."

That seemed to catch her off guard. Her smirk faltered for a beat.

"Okay. Noted. Broody, maybe-human tech guy. Virgo. Probably sleeps in spreadsheets."

I arched a brow. "And you? Or do I just assume the barefoot Bond girl twirling through my living room isn't the real threat here?"

Her face lit up like I'd handed her a trophy. "Did you just call me a Bond girl?"

"I meant assassin."

She waved a hand. "Still counts."

Of course it did.

She stood, struck a pose, and gestured like cameras were rolling. "Mia Wilder. Product designer. Sagittarius. Chaos in a cute wrapper. Also? Not a serial killer. Recovering perfectionist with a caffeine dependency and a tendency to monologue under pressure."

I blinked.

She grinned. "And no, I'm not always like this. Sometimes I'm worse."

I looked at her. At the sarong. The wild hair. The hurricane energy wrapped in sun-kissed skin.

Then I reached for a chair.

Because apparently, I was going to need to sit down.

Chapter Three

MIA

HE SAT DOWN LIKE my entire personality physically exhausted him.

Which—rude.

I mean, I'd just delivered a deluxe introduction: charm, facts, sparkle rating solidly nine out of ten. The least he could do was pretend to be impressed instead of staring at me like I was a walking migraine in a pink sarong.

Classic grump.

He sat. I hovered. Not because I was nervous—please—I *thrive* in chaos. I just needed a minute to recalibrate. To mentally map out how one survives being stranded with a hot, emotionally constipated tech billionaire whose idea of vulnerability is switching to decaf.

"So," I said, hands on hips. "Ground rules."

Grant Ashford looked up like I'd suggested a corporate trust fall.

"Rules," he repeated flatly.

"Yes. We're two strangers stuck on an island in a storm. One bungalow. One bed. High potential for emotional implosion. We need parameters."

He just stared at me.

"Sleeping arrangements," I added. "You get the couch. Obviously."

His brow lifted. Dangerously slow. "Why is that obvious?"

"I was here first. And I already flopped on the bed, which makes it mine by squatter's rights."

He pinched the bridge of his nose like I'd caused him physical pain. "Fine. You get the bed."

"Thank you." I gave him a gracious nod. "Next: bathroom etiquette. Closed door means knock. Open door also means knock. Touch my skincare, and I'll hex you."

Flat stare. "I brought my own."

"Well," I said, flopping into the armchair, "look at Mr. Self-Sufficient. I can tell we're going to be best friends."

He didn't respond. Just leaned back with his arms crossed like he was silently calculating how long he could survive before the storm—or I—broke him.

I squinted at him. Not threateningly—scientifically.

He looked like someone who color-coded his inbox and ironed his socks. Under all that broody control-freak energy? Annoyingly, objectively hot.

"You know," I said, tilting my head, "you give off serious 'my calendar is optimized for maximum efficiency' vibes."

Nothing.

"Do you have a spreadsheet for emotional regulation? A pie chart for trust issues?"

Still nothing. Was he rebooting?

I waved a hand. "Hello? Earth to Grant. I'm trying to bond here."

He sighed—long, suffering, the kind you save for dental appointments and DMV lines.

"Right," I muttered. "Best friends it is."

I stood. I needed a break. From the silence. From the tension. From the way he looked at me like I was a pop-up ad he couldn't close.

"I'm going to assess the storm," I declared. "You stay here and continue brooding into the furniture."

He stood too—probably to argue—but thought better of it.

I marched to the door, flung it open like I was personally in charge of the weather—and got slammed in the face with wind.

The wind howled, and my hair whipped around like it was auditioning for a shampoo commercial. My sarong took flight. And a second later, it smacked into Grant like some sort of pastel heat-seeking missile. It hit him square in the chest, wrapped once around his shoulder like a very confused fashion statement, and just... stayed there.

He didn't move. Just stared down at the fabric clinging to his chest.

Then—very slowly—he lifted his eyes to me.

"Was this part of the rules?" he asked, deadpan. "Or are we improvising now?"

"ARE YOU KIDDING ME?" I shrieked, slamming the door and pointing at him like he'd just committed a felony.

He looked down at the fabric stuck to him. One brow arched.

"You lost something," he said.

"I KNOW," I snapped. "I was *wearing* that!"

His gaze dragged down my now-sarongless body, lingering just long enough to make my skin buzz.

"So I noticed," he said calmly. "Hard not to."

I made a strangled sound, lunged forward, and yanked the sarong from his shoulder like it had betrayed me.

"I hate everything," I muttered, rewrapping it with the grace of someone losing a fight with humidity and pride.

He didn't laugh.

But the look on his face?

That smug, not-quite-smile?

Absolutely weaponized.

GRANT

I wasn't proud of it, but I forgot how to speak for a second.

She shrieked, snatched the sarong like it had committed a felony, and rewrapped herself with all the flustered dignity of a woman wronged by the weather.

And I just stood there. Frozen. Not laughing. But God help me—I wanted to.

The glare. The blush. The way her hands fumbled with fabric like it owed her an apology.

Ridiculous.

And... stunning.

Not the kind of polished, posed beauty I saw at charity galas and launch events. No, Mia was barefoot chaos. Sun-kissed skin, windblown curls, and a spark in her eyes that dared the world to keep up. A woman designed by nature to dismantle structure.

I turned to the kitchen. I needed cold. I needed order. I needed the fridge.

I opened it like it might give me clarity and stared at an overly curated lineup of juices, herbs, and artisanal bottled water.

None of it helped.

Across the room, she was muttering to herself while re-arranging the welcome fruit like it had personally wronged her.

"Papaya," she said, nudging it like a grudge. "Statement fruit. Nobody eats it unless they're trying to prove something."

She adjusted a banana. Eyed the pineapple like it had spoken out of turn.

"Too much citrus in one corner. Amateur move. Basic fruit feng shui."

I stared out the window, trying to out-storm the storm. Rain blurred the view. Wind howled like it was insulted. The palm trees bent at angles that seemed medically un-wise.

Still no help.

Then, blessedly, silence.

"What are you doing?" she asked behind me.

"Reevaluating my definition of 'vacation,'" I muttered.

She made a noise—somewhere between a laugh and a groan. "Great. So. What's for dinner?"

I blinked, looked over my shoulder. She was perched on the couch's arm like a gremlin in vacation mode, eyebrows lifted like she expected an actual answer.

"You think I'm cooking?"

"I'm not," she said brightly. "I'm in vacation mode. I don't cook in vacation mode."

"Do you cook out of vacation mode?"

"Not if I can help it."

I sighed and reopened the fridge with the resignation of a man preparing to wage war against a gourmet grocery haul.

"Wagyu filet. Truffle butter. Three kinds of heirloom carrots. Who the hell stocks this stuff?"

She let out a delighted gasp. "This fridge is fancier than my last relationship."

I didn't turn. "That's a low bar."

"Excuse you. It was a very decorative relationship. Zero substance. High aesthetic."

I almost smiled.

Almost.

Still staring into the fridge, I said, "At least we won't starve."

"You're doing great," she chirped.

I turned. "You could help."

"I *am* helping. With morale. I'm the vibe manager."

I handed her a cutting board. She blinked at it.

"I don't chop," she said. "I curate."

"Then curate the carrots. By height, color, emotional baggage. Dealer's choice."

She grinned. "Height and mood. Obviously."

And somehow, we were cooking together.

Quiet. Almost comfortable.

The knives tapped gently against the counter. Outside, the storm kept roaring, but in here—it was calm. As calm as it could be with Mia narrating the emotional backstory of every herb.

I'd cooked with people before—on dates, at events, while making polite conversation. But this? This felt different.

Close.

Familiar in a way that had no right to feel familiar.

Her shoulder brushed mine. Her laugh skimmed over my skin. I caught myself watching her hands instead of the knife.

I turned my focus to the steak.

Because I didn't come here for this.

And I really wasn't ready for how easy she made it feel.

Chapter Four

Mia

"THIS IS DELICIOUS," I declared, closing my eyes like I was on a cooking show. "Perfect sear. Subtle seasoning. A delicate whisper of truffle. Honestly, I should be on the Food Network by now."

Grant looked at me over his wine glass. "You cut two carrots."

"And arranged them artfully," I said, gesturing to the plates like I was unveiling a museum exhibit. "Plating is half the experience."

He didn't argue—just returned to his steak like being casually excellent was his default setting.

I stabbed a carrot, chewed thoughtfully, then pointed my fork at him. "So, Mr. Broody Tech Billionaire Virgo, why are you here?"

He glanced at the window, where the wind whipped the palm trees like it had a vendetta. "Storm. Wrong bungalow. Trapped by weather. General chaos."

I rolled my eyes. "Not physically here. I mean why *here* here—this island. No people. No Wi-Fi. No DoorDash."

He set down his knife, took a sip of wine, and stared at the table like weighing his answer against the likelihood I'd make another papaya joke.

Finally, he said, "I needed quiet."

"From what?"

A beat. Then: "Everything. My company. My calendar. The constant noise of being needed."

I nodded, chewing slower. "So you came to detox from humanity."

He looked at me, meeting my eyes for real this time. "Basically."

"And then you got me," I said with a grin.

That earned the tiniest twitch at the corner of his mouth. "Basically."

I leaned forward, fork still in hand. "So let me get this straight—you came out here for monk-level solitude... and instead got a surprise plus-one who talks too much, claims half the bungalow by force of personality, and has zero respect for your existential brooding?"

He arched a brow. "That's one way to put it."

"I'm an acquired taste," I said, swirling my wine. "Like olives. Or socks with sandals. Once you're in, though—very on trend."

He shook his head, but the almost-smile was still there.

"Ironically," I added, "I came here for the same reason."

His brows lifted. "You?"

"Shocking, I know. But yes. I, Mia Wilder—chaotic, caffeinated, allegedly allergic to stillness—needed quiet, too."

I tapped my fingers against my glass. "I was tired of always doing, fixing, being everything for everyone. I wanted stillness. A hammock. A hard reset."

He didn't speak at first. Just watched me with something softer in his eyes. Something that made me feel... understood.

"Guess we picked the wrong island," he said.

"Or," I nudged his foot lightly under the table, "the universe picked the right one. We just haven't figured out why yet."

He didn't pull away. But he didn't answer either.

The silence stretched, but it felt full. Not awkward. Like a story waiting to begin.

We stood together, wine warm in our cheeks. I reached for my plate just as he reached for his, our hands brushing.

Just a spark.

Nothing major.

Definitely nothing I'd overanalyze later. Probably.

"Thanks for cooking," I said. "And for not insulting my expert carrot placement."

"I didn't say I wasn't judging," he said, voice low, amused.

I made it halfway to the sink before it happened.

BOOM.

Thunder cracked, sharp and loud. The windows rattled. The lights flickered.

And just like that—pitch black.

I screamed.

Not dramatically.

Okay, dramatically.

Before realizing what I was doing, I'd launched myself across the kitchen like a flying squirrel and *latched* onto Grant.

"JESUS, TAKE THE WHEEL," I shrieked, full koala mode, arms and legs wrapped around him like he was the last tree in a lightning storm.

He didn't fall.

Didn't stumble.

Just... stood there. Solid. Warm. Unreasonably calm.

"Darkness," I gasped against his neck. "Unnatural. Terrifying. Betrayal by electricity."

His hands were hovering like he didn't quite know what to do with me. "Are you—are you afraid of the dark?"

"No," I said, clearly lying. "I'm afraid of—uh—*surprise ambiance.*"

He made a low, strangled sound that might have been a laugh. "You jumped on me like I was a life raft."

"Don't flatter yourself," I muttered, not moving. "You're tall and sturdy. This is purely survival instinct."

Grant shifted slightly, and I realized I was still clinging to him like a wind-chime in a hurricane.

"I'm going to set you down now," he said, voice dry.

"Fine," I huffed, loosening my grip. "But if something jumps out of the shadows, I'm climbing back up."

GRANT

One second, I was clearing the table.

The next, she was wrapped around me like I'd just pulled her from a burning building—arms around my neck, legs around my waist, face pressed against my throat. A human exclamation point who smelled like coconut and chaos.

And my body?

Fully betraying me.

A bolt of heat shot through me, and my hands—traitorous—found her hips. Steadying her. Anchoring her. Not because I meant to. Just because she was there, and I was a man, and she was—

God.

Soft. Warm. Maddening. From her frantic breathing to the way she muttered like the storm owed her money.

I'd come here for peace. Stillness.

Not this.

But here she was, clinging to me like I was the only thing keeping her grounded. And my body responded like it had been waiting for her all along.

Unacceptable. Unsettling. Unavoidable.

"I'm going to set you down now," I said, my voice rougher than I intended.

She huffed something vaguely threatening and loosened her grip. I set her down, hands lingering longer than they should've.

The moment she stepped back, the air felt colder.

She crossed her arms. "That wasn't a scream, by the way. It was a—battle cry."

"Of course it was," I muttered, turning to grab the emergency candles before I started thinking about how good she'd felt in my arms.

The match flared. Light hit her face—wide-eyed, flushed, lips parted like she still hadn't caught her breath.

Neither had I.

The match burned too close. I swore softly and shook it out.

Lit another. Soft glow. Long shadows. The bungalow looked different like this. Quieter. Intimate. Like it was holding its breath.

So was I.

She watched me pretending not to. When I handed her a candle, she raised a brow. "So this is what we're working with?"

"Seems like it."

She nodded. "Not the worst lighting I've seen."

"Glad it meets your standards."

I moved into the living room. She followed, her bare feet whispering across the floor.

The silence returned—but it wasn't peaceful. It was the kind that made everything louder in my head.

The soft rustle of her steps. The way her hair caught the candlelight. That barely-there smile she didn't know she was wearing.

"Okay," she said, slicing through the silence. "We're officially one thunderclap away from romantic horror movie territory. Love that for us."

I huffed a laugh and lit the last candle.

She was close.

Too close.

And I didn't move.

Neither did she.

She studied me like she couldn't decide if I was fascinating or infuriating. Odds were even.

The candlelight softened everything—edges, shadows, restraint.

Bad idea.

"You okay?" she asked.

I nodded. Too tight. The kind of nod you give when you're lying to everyone, including yourself.

"You sure?" she pressed, voice low. "You look like you're either solving a math problem or plotting an escape."

"Little of both," I muttered.

She laughed.

Not polite. Not forced.

Real. Warm.

And just like that, I was wrecked.

The feeling hit low and hard, curling through me like something I'd been avoiding for years.

I stepped back. Useless.

"We should probably call it a night," I said, keeping my voice neutral. "Long travel day. Hopefully the storm clears and we can figure out whatever booking glitch landed us in the same GPS coordinates."

She nodded. "Sleep. Great idea." Then perked up. "Bathroom first?"

I gestured toward the hall. "Be my guest."

She lifted her candle like she was leading a séance and swept off with dramatic solemnity. "If I'm not back in ten minutes, assume the storm swallowed me whole."

"If you disappear, I'm claiming the bed," I called after her.

Ten minutes later, she returned—hair in a bun, skin shiny from whatever ritual had just taken place.

"Your turn," she said, handing over the candle like it was sacred.

The bathroom smelled like coconut and something botanical I didn't want to think about too hard.

When I came back, she was frowning at the candles.

"We probably shouldn't leave these burning," she said. "Unless you want to wake up in a luxury bonfire."

Fair.

I snuffed them out one by one. The room dimmed with every puff.

"I left you a blanket and pillow," she added, already retreating toward the bedroom. "No booby traps."

"Appreciated."

"Oh—and I get the bathroom first in the morning."

"Noted."

She paused in the doorway, glanced back. "Night, Grant."

"Night, Mia."

The door clicked shut.

And then it was just me. The dark. The storm.

And the lingering scent of coconut.

Chapter Five

MIA

I WAS FINE.

Totally, absolutely, one hundred percent fine.

Just a woman in a luxury bungalow, curled up in a bed the size of a small country, trying not to flinch every time the storm tested the structural integrity of the roof.

Fine.

Lightning flashed. Thunder cracked loud enough to shake the windows. My pulse sprinted.

"Okay," I whispered to the ceiling, "maybe not fine-fine. More like... functional fine."

I yanked the blanket up to my chin.

The wind shrieked. Something thudded. Something else creaked. I squeaked.

This was ridiculous. I was Mia Wilder—independent, overcaffeinated, chaos-certified—but I'd survived worse.

Corporate meltdowns. Artistic burnout. That tequila-fueled birthday in Cabo.

Surely I could handle a little atmospheric drama.

Unless the dark came with ghost noises and judgmental bungalow groans.

I flipped over. Then back. Then again.

Blanket off. Blanket on. Blanket off.

I glared at the ceiling. "This is fine. This is totally, completely—"

BOOM.

That one shook the bed.

I sat up, hair sticking out like an electrocuted hedgehog.

Absolutely not. No way. I was not asking him. I would sooner hold a séance to summon my own emotional support ghost.

I threw off the covers.

Thirty seconds later, I padded down the hallway in my oversized sleep shirt, bun a mess, holding a candle like I was about to summon spirits.

I paused at the edge of the living room.

Grant lay stretched out on the couch—bare chest, broad shoulders, and all six feet of broody logic in one deeply inconvenient package.

This was a mistake.

I was not doing this.

Except I totally was.

I cleared my throat.

He shifted but didn't open his eyes. "You good?"

"Define good."

One eye cracked open. He blinked, then slowly sat up. "What's wrong?"

I clutched the candle tighter. "Okay. So. Hypothetically... if someone—me—were slightly, mildly, extremely freaked out by the darkness and the horror movie happening outside... would it be the worst thing if that someone asked you to maybe sleep in the same room?"

Silence.

"I mean, it's a huge bed," I added quickly. "We'd have our own zip codes. I wouldn't even notice unless you started snoring in binary."

Still nothing.

"Or not," I backpedaled. "Totally fine. I can go back. Curl up with the throw pillows and my crushing sense of shame. That works too."

Another crack of thunder.

Grant stood.

No words. No grumbling. Not even a sigh.

He just grabbed his pillow and walked past me—silent, solid, and unfairly steady as the wind howled like a banshee behind us.

I followed like a guilty toddler.

Inside the bedroom, the candle cast long shadows. He paused at the foot of the bed like he was doing spatial calculations.

"This thing's massive," he muttered.

"Right?" I whispered, like the bed might be flattered. "Enough space for three awkward coworkers and a life coach."

He shook his head and walked around to the far side.

I scrambled to mine, threw myself under the covers, and tried to act casual.

Totally chill. Not at all aware that the hot, emotionally reserved tech guy was now adjusting a pillow on the same mattress.

Still shirtless, he lay back with a long exhale.

Neither of us spoke. The candle flickered on the nightstand. The storm growled outside.

The air felt... still.

"Thanks," I whispered.

"For what?"

"For not laughing. Or calling me ridiculous. Or ignoring me completely."

A pause. Then, "You're not ridiculous."

"Wow," I said. "Compliment accepted. Writing that in my mental scrapbook."

Another pause.

"You're just... loud."

I snorted into the pillow. "And you're emotionally constipated."

He didn't deny it.

Thunder rolled again.

But this time, I didn't flinch.

Maybe because he was here.

Maybe because he didn't feel like the kind of guy who'd let the storm get in.

"I don't snore," he said suddenly.

I turned my head. "What?"

"You said something about binary snoring."

"Oh. Right." I smiled. "Good to know."

A beat.

"Do you?"

"Snore?" I lifted a brow. "Only if I've had dairy. Or spent the day suppressing emotional turmoil."

"So... yes."

I grinned into the dark. "Goodnight, Grant."

He was quiet for a second.

Then: "Goodnight, Mia."

GRANT

This wasn't how I pictured the week going.

I came for silence. For space. For a break from being the guy who fixed everything.

Instead, I got her.

Mia Wilder—curled up on the opposite side of the bed like it was hers by right. One foot kicked out from beneath the covers. Her hair was a halo of chaos across the pillow. Breathing even. Shoulders finally relaxed.

Not asleep. Not yet. But close.

The storm still roared outside, but she wasn't flinching anymore.

Because I was here.

And that shouldn't have made something tighten in my chest.

I turned onto my back and stared at the ceiling. The battery-powered candle I'd found glowed on the nightstand, casting soft shadows and too much clarity.

I could see her.

The curve of her shoulder. The freckle near her collarbone. Her parted lips, her quiet breath. I could still feel her clinging to me earlier—legs, arms, voice in my ear like I was the only solid thing in a storm.

It wasn't just that she was beautiful—though, God, she was. It was the way she existed. Loud. Unfiltered. Fearless.

Like the world was hers to narrate and bend into something brighter.

She was chaos.

And I did not do chaos.

I did order. Discipline. Control. That's how I built everything that mattered.

So why the hell was I lying next to a human supernova, wide awake, and not thinking about any of that?

I closed my eyes. I wasn't going to touch her. Wasn't going to move. I'd sleep. Wait out the storm.

That was the plan.

But it wasn't just physical anymore.

It was her laugh in the kitchen. Her battle cries over fruit. The way she made me forget about deadlines and deliverables and the gnawing ache of never being enough.

I must've drifted off somewhere between denial and resignation.

And then—

I was dreaming.

Sunlight filtered through open doors. A breeze carried the scent of citrus and salt. Mia danced barefoot in the kitchen, wearing an oversized white button-down that barely hit mid-thigh. Her hair was a mess. Her smile was not.

She twirled around the floor like it was a stage, claiming the room with narration I didn't understand but never wanted to stop hearing.

And then she was walking toward me.

Slow. Intentional.

Her eyes locked on mine—challenging, curious, unafraid.

She reached up, fingers brushing my collarbone, pausing there.

"I think the universe knew what it was doing," she whispered.

Then her mouth touched mine.

Soft. Testing.

And I broke.

I kissed her like she was the only thing tethering me to earth. Like I'd been waiting for this without knowing it. Her hands slid under my shirt. Mine found her waist, her back, the shape of her.

"Grant," she gasped—and it undid me.

I lifted her, carried her to the bed, laid her down like she was holy.

She looked up at me, laughing, wild, radiant.

I leaned in.

CRACK.

Thunder split the sky.

I jolted awake, heart pounding.

The candle still glowed. The storm still screamed. And Mia was still beside me, turned away, blanket curled tight.

The dream was gone.

But the feeling?

That stayed.

It wasn't just the kiss I didn't want to lose. It was what came with it—the wake-up call. The pull. The terrifying, magnetic realization that something in me had shifted.

And she was the reason.

I wasn't sleeping again. Not now. Not with her so close and the storm still howling—outside, and in me.

Quietly, I slid out of bed and headed for the living room.

Chapter Six

MIA

I woke up warm.

Which, considering the storm still sounded like it was auditioning for the apocalypse, was unexpected.

The bed was soft. The blanket cocoon-level cozy. For one blissful second, I just floated—half-asleep, half-aware.

Then I noticed it.

Something was missing.

Someone.

I opened one eye, then the other. Grant's side of the bed was empty.

His pillow was faintly indented. The covers slightly rumpled. But no broody CEO in sight.

Bathroom?

Nope. The door was cracked open, dark. The soft flicker of a battery-powered candle glowed in the corner.

I sat up, heart doing that weird stutter-step it saved for moments when spiraling was imminent. He probably just needed air. Or space. Or a moment to regret this whole situation in silence.

Still...

I grabbed a candle and padded into the living room.

There he was—Grant, sitting on the couch, elbows on his knees, head bowed like the weight of something he hadn't figured out yet was sitting right there with him. Candlelight carved shadows across his face, sharp and unreadable.

He hadn't heard me.

Which meant I had five seconds to either turn around or admit I already missed him beside me.

"You okay?" I asked, voice softer than I meant it to be.

His head lifted slowly, eyes finding mine—and something in my chest stuttered again.

It wasn't just the look.

It was the heat behind it.

Like he'd been thinking about me. Still was.

Suddenly, I was acutely aware I was wearing nothing but an oversized sleep shirt, barefoot, holding a flickering candle like I was auditioning for a gothic romance reboot.

"Couldn't sleep?" I asked.

He didn't answer right away. Just kept looking at me like I'd short-circuited something vital.

"Not really," he said finally, voice rough.

"Yeah," I said, stepping closer. "Me either."

The air shifted—soft and electric.

Something was happening.

"I didn't mean to wake you," he added.

"You didn't," I lied.

I sat at the other end of the couch. Close, but not touching.

He glanced over. "I don't know what to do with this."

"This?"

"You," he said. "This. Us. Whatever the hell this is."

I froze.

"You're chaos," he continued. "And I don't mean that as an insult."

I arched a brow. "Flattering start."

"You're loud. Bright. Unpredictable. You narrate everything. You argue with produce. You fill a room and don't apologize for it."

"Sounds exhausting," I said.

"It is," he agreed. "And yet I can't stop thinking about you."

My heart caught.

"I came here to clear my head. Not to—" His gaze dropped to my mouth. "Not to want someone."

Oh.

"You're everything I'm not—chaotic where I'm controlled, fire where I'm logic. And somehow, instead of pushing me away, it's what's pulling me in."

The silence pulsed between us.

"There's no algorithm for this," he said. "No logic. But since the second I saw you spinning in the kitchen like a hurricane, it hasn't stopped."

I swallowed. "You're trying to logic your way out of liking me."

"I'm trying to understand it," he said hoarsely. "Because I don't jump without a plan."

I leaned in, just enough to almost touch. "Maybe this doesn't need a plan. Maybe it just is."

He didn't move.

So I did.

Close enough to see the candlelight flicker in his eyes. "For the record," I whispered, "I'm not asking for answers. Just honesty. And maybe a little bravery."

He stared at me like I'd rewritten his code in real time.

"I don't fall fast," he said. "But I dreamt about you just now."

I blinked. "Dreamt?"

He nodded. "You were dancing in the kitchen. Wearing my shirt."

My breath caught.

"Laughing like you always do. Like you've never been afraid."

And just like that, the floor tilted.

Maybe because I felt it too—the gravity shift. The impossibility of what was happening.

So I said quietly:

"Maybe the universe isn't trying to make sense. Maybe it's trying to wake you up."

His gaze dropped to my lips.

"Do you really believe that?" he asked.

"I don't know," I said with a smile. "But I really want to. And I'm kind of hoping you'll stop overthinking long enough to find out."

GRANT

I couldn't think. And I couldn't *not* think. She was too close, too bright—and I wanted her.

"I want you," I said, voice rough.

She leaned back slightly, surprise flashing across her face before a wicked smile took over. "Really?" she whispered. "Because that's exactly what I was hoping for."

That was all it took.

I moved without thinking, closing the space between us in a heartbeat. Her mouth found mine—sharp, sweet, hungry. Her hands slid into my hair like they belonged there. Mine landed on her waist, pulling her into my lap. She settled easily, like this had always been the plan.

I kissed her again, deeper, harder, and she gasped against me.

"Grant," she breathed, wide-eyed, breathless, alive in a way that made my chest ache.

And then—because of course—it was Mia. She laughed. That brilliant, uncontainable laugh that cracked open something in me.

I kissed her again to keep from saying something I'd regret. Or maybe something I wouldn't.

I hadn't known how much I wanted her until she was pressed against me, straddling my lap, her body melting into mine like we'd done this a hundred times.

It was reckless. It was real.

And I didn't care.

Mia Wilder had turned my world upside down in a matter of hours, and I wasn't pretending anymore.

Her mouth on mine was fire and mischief. She shifted in my lap, and a low sound escaped me—half groan, half plea.

She pulled back just enough to smirk. "For a broody CEO, you're surprisingly good at team-building."

I almost laughed. Almost.

"This is insane," she said, eyes dancing.

"Completely."

"I'm not usually this easy."

"Neither am I."

And just like that, she moved again—slow, purposeful—and any thought of restraint vanished.

"Keep doing that," I said, breath catching. "And we're not making it to the bed."

She didn't stop.

Her hands slid up my chest, mouth hot on mine, body pressed close enough to make thought impossible. She broke the kiss to reach for the hem of her oversized shirt.

"Too fast?" she asked softly.

Then the shirt was gone—and so was my sanity.

I swore under my breath. "Not fast enough."

She laughed, low and wicked, and leaned back in. My hands roamed her skin, committing every inch to memory. Her waist, her back, her hips—soft, warm, perfect.

She kissed me again—wild and sweet and unfiltered.

And then she slid off my lap and onto the floor, kneeling between my knees.

My breath caught hard.

She looked up at me, candlelight flickering in her eyes, her hands sliding slowly up my thighs like she already knew what she was doing to me. Or maybe she just liked watching me fall apart.

"Mia," I said—rough, low, already gone.

She hooked her fingers into the waistband of my shorts and tugged.

I sucked in a breath as she wrapped one hand around me, squeezing lightly. Heat shot through me like a live wire. Like nothing I'd felt before.

I was gone.

Completely lost in the way she touched me, the way she looked at me like I was something to devour. Like I'd been hers for far longer than one chaotic night.

She lowered her mouth, and my whole world went white. Hot. Real.

Her mouth—God, her mouth was warm and wet, and I might've actually blacked out for a second.

The first stroke was slow and deliberate. My head fell back, and I swore. Loudly.

"Jesus," I hissed, pure sensation hitting me like a tidal wave.

Her tongue, her lips, the slow drag of heat—it was too much. It wasn't enough. It was everything.

My hands tangled in her hair, holding on like I might come apart otherwise.

She set a pace that unraveled me, each stroke and glide sending pleasure sparking through nerves I didn't know I had. My pulse pounded in time with every move—urgent, wild, and entirely out of control.

She hollowed her cheeks, and my hips bucked.

"Mia," I groaned, voice ragged and raw. "God."

I was breaking, undone in the best possible way. Completely, utterly wrecked.

And then she went deeper—took more—and the bottom dropped out of my world.

I let out a sharp sound, my body tensing hard as release tore through me fast and fierce. My vision blurred. My grip tightened in her hair as waves of heat rolled through every inch of skin and bone, long and unrelenting.

For a second, I forgot how to breathe.

Then she eased up slowly, her touch gentle and reverent as I returned to myself. As my pulse stopped, trying to set new speed records. As my mind caught up with my body, I realized what had just happened. Holy shit.

I let out a shaky breath.

Everything felt unsteady in the best possible way.

Mia leaned back on her heels, eyes bright and wicked in the candlelight. She looked like chaos and desire and victory. Like she knew exactly what she'd done.

Like she loved every second.

A slow smile curved her mouth as she knelt there.

I reached for her.

She didn't resist—just let me pull her back into my lap, soft and satisfied and somehow even more dangerous than before.

My hands slid up her back, hungry for more.

"Your turn," I murmured against her throat.

Chapter Seven

MIA

GRANT EASED ME TO the edge of the couch and knelt between my legs.

Then his mouth closed over my nipple—kissing, teasing, then grazing it with his teeth—and I shattered.

"Grant," I gasped, arching into him.

He made a low sound that vibrated through me, then shifted to the other breast, tongue stroking in slow, maddening circles until I was a mess beneath him.

His mouth moved lower, trailing heat down my stomach until he reached the waistband of my thong. His breath hit my skin—and I was already gone.

He glanced up, eyes dark with intent, then kissed me through the lace.

My hips bucked. My pulse spiked. The friction was electric.

I cried out—raw, wild, completely undone—and he didn't stop. He just deepened the pressure, licking through the fabric with relentless, knowing precision.

By the time I realized the thong was gone, his mouth was back—bare, direct, devastating.

White-hot urgency built fast—too fast—but I couldn't stop it. Couldn't slow down. Couldn't do anything but gasp his name and hope I survived this intact.

"Grant," I panted as his tongue circled and teased, "Oh my God."

I was a live wire. A frayed end. A spark about to ignite.

And then he slid two fingers inside me, and I exploded.

The world went bright, then dark, then bright again as pleasure crashed over me in a dizzying wave. I heard myself moan, loud and long and completely undone.

His mouth didn't stop—he kept stroking as I shattered around him, pulling every last bit of sensation from my body.

It was too much. It was nowhere near enough.

I was still trembling when he finally eased up, both of us breathing hard in the candlelit dark.

"Wow." The word came out on a breathless laugh. "For a broody CEO, you really don't cut corners."

He grinned against my thigh. "I pride myself on being thorough."

I pulled him up to me, desperate for more contact, for another taste of the man who'd just destroyed me in the best possible way.

His mouth covered mine—hot and demanding—and I could taste myself on his lips. It sent another jolt through me.

He kissed me like he was starving, rolling us so I was straddling him again, skin against skin.

I broke the kiss, breathless. "Is this too much? I mean—do you need a minute? Or can we—?"

Grant flipped us, pinning me beneath him, already hard against my thigh.

"Trust me," he said roughly, "I'm ready."

I wrapped my legs around him—but he froze.

"What?" I asked.

He blinked. "Condoms. I didn't bring any."

I groaned. "Seriously?"

"I wasn't planning for this."

"Neither was I." I sat up, brushing hair out of my face. "You were not part of my relaxation itinerary."

He muttered something under his breath, glancing toward the bedroom. "Maybe the resort included... essentials."

"Emergency romance supplies?" I was already up, candle in hand. "Let's find out."

I grabbed the candle and sprinted to the bedroom, flinging open drawers like a prize was at the bottom of each.

"Bingo!" I yelled, holding up a foil packet. Then two. "We're officially saved!"

Grant sat up, looking equal parts turned on and relieved.

I shut the door behind me, climbed into his lap, and handed him one.

He opened it with his teeth—of course—and rolled it on with practiced focus that nearly broke me all over again.

"I want you," he said, voice low as he lifted me.

One smooth thrust and he was inside me—hot, thick, perfect.

"Grant!" I gasped, rocking against him, pulse spiking as the pressure built with each slow, perfect stroke.

His hands gripped my hips, guiding me and setting a rhythm that made it clear neither of us would last long. Desperate sounds escaped my mouth with every move—his name, my breath—a wild symphony in the quiet.

"God," he groaned, eyes dark as they watched me ride him. "Mia."

Hearing my name on his lips did it—I shattered again, harder than before, breaking apart around him with a cry.

He followed fast—a low, deep sound tearing from his throat as he drove into me one last time. His release hit hard enough that I could feel it even through the condom, an electric pulse through my core.

We stayed tangled together, chests heaving, skin slick, hearts pounding like they were racing each other.

Neither of us moved.

GRANT

We stayed like that—tangled, silent, real. The storm still howled outside, but for the first time, it didn't matter.

Eventually, we moved. Just long enough to clean up, crawl into bed, and remember how to breathe.

Mia curled into me, her hair wild against my chest, the blanket pulled over us like a truce with the world. I traced the curve of her shoulder, breathing in the warm, unmistakable scent of us.

"Wow," she murmured on a soft exhale. "The universe really knows how to crash a vacation."

"Not complaining," I said into her hair.

She hummed. "So... fate? Or just two stranded people with very good timing?"

I didn't answer right away. Her skin was warm, her breath a whisper against my neck.

"I think it doesn't matter what it's called," I said quietly.

She shifted, lifting her face just enough to meet my gaze.

"We're here," I added. "And that's enough."

She smiled.

So I kissed her—slow, deep, unhurried. Like we had all night. Like there was no world outside this room.

But my body had other ideas.

It surged back to life with a speed that surprised even me, pulling her closer like it couldn't bear to let her go.

Mia laughed softly against my mouth. "Do you ever run out of batteries?"

I pulled back just enough to meet her eyes. "You're one to talk."

Then I flipped her onto her stomach with one smooth motion.

She was quick to catch on, her hips lifting, back arching as I slid behind her.

The view was incredible. She was incredible. I quickly slipped on another condom and traced a line down her spine, my pulse racing to keep up with the rest of me.

Mia made a low, impatient, and urgent sound, so I gave us exactly what we wanted.

One deep thrust and I was inside her again—deep and breathless and sinking into the kind of heat that made every single thought disappear except this one: How had I survived this long without her?

She let out a sharp moan, pushing back against me with a rhythm that was pure instinct. Pure need. Her hand tangled in the sheets. Her hair tumbled over one bare shoulder. Her skin was gold against the candlelight, her body warm and alive beneath mine.

Jesus Christ.

I picked up the pace, each thrust taking us closer to the edge. Mia's breaths turned ragged—the kind of gasps that would ruin me if they hadn't already.

"Grant," she panted, voice barely there but everything I needed to hear.

I shifted slightly, changing the angle until she cried out and dropped her head against the pillow. Until nothing else mattered except our breath and bodies and how goddamn good this felt.

I wanted this forever. Wanted her forever.

The thought hit hard—fast enough to have me tensing as release slammed through, fast enough to have me clenching my jaw as she shattered again beneath me, a low groan escaping my throat as I followed right behind her with a final thrust.

We collapsed forward together, her hair spilling across my chest, both of us breathing hard and not moving for a long time.

We stayed like that—breathless and tangled with the storm, her heartbeat under my hand and mine under hers. I should have been exhausted. Or worried. Or making a mental list of all the ways this would explode in my face when the real world caught up.

But somehow, I wasn't.

Somehow, I didn't care.

There'd be time for questions later. For logic, labels, and all the things we were supposed to talk about but hadn't yet.

But not tonight.

Tonight, I was going to let this be what it was. Real. Unexpected. Exactly where I wanted to be.

I pulled her closer.

She made a soft sound in her sleep, curling into me like she already knew how this story ended.

And for once, I wasn't in a rush to find out.

So I closed my eyes.

And let myself rest.

Chapter Eight

MIA

I WOKE UP TO gray skies and Grant's hand on my ass.

To be fair—it was a very nice hand. And clearly confident in its new home, resting warm and solid against bare skin like it had no intention of relocating.

I didn't hate it.

Stretching slightly, I felt the delicious ache of muscles thoroughly used in... every way possible. The blanket shifted, but Grant didn't stir—just made a low, sleepy sound that went straight to my core and tightened his grip.

So that's how it was going to be.

I burrowed closer, a smile tugging at my lips. The storm had eased—not gone, but no longer threatening to launch us into the ocean. Which, considering the total lack of clothing, would've made for an awkward evacuation.

And what a night.

The memory made me grin. Still vivid, still electric. My body buzzed in all the best ways, my heart doing this odd little tap dance, and my brain? Absolutely no use to me.

I shifted to look at him.

Rumpled hair, slack jaw, faintest smile like the night had followed him into his dreams. He looked peaceful. Vulnerable. Like maybe he'd stay here forever if no one reminded him of the real world.

A reckless little voice whispered that maybe he could stay right here instead.

I pressed a soft kiss to his chest—no expectations, just... thanks. Just warmth.

He stirred, muttered something incoherent, then blinked awake—slow and disoriented but still, unfairly, stupidly attractive.

"Hey there, sleepy CEO," I teased. "We survived. The storm. The night. Each other. Barely."

His arm tightened around me, but his smile didn't quite reach his eyes. "Morning."

"Well," I said lightly, "I can officially cross 'unexpected island fling' off my bucket list."

It was a joke. A harmless deflection. Something breezy to ease the swirl of too many feelings I wasn't ready to name.

But something shifted in Grant.

Not big. Not obvious. Just enough to register like a flicker in the light.

He didn't tense. Didn't flinch.

He just... went still.

His arm, once wrapped around me, loosened. His hand drifted from my skin like he'd suddenly remembered where we were.

When he finally spoke, his voice was quiet. Neutral.

"Right. Guess that's one way to look at it."

And just like that, the warmth cracked.

Barely. But enough.

Maybe it was nothing. Maybe he was tired. Processing. Already mentally triaging his inbox. But I felt the space open up between us—small but unmistakable.

I tried again.

"Technically, I should probably also cross off 'survive a tropical storm,' but that feels less impressive."

He made a noncommittal sound. Not a laugh. Not even close.

I glanced over.

He was sitting up now, the sheet around his waist, back turned to me as he reached for a glass of water. Every movement was calm. Measured. Polite.

Like he was rehearsing distance.

"I'm gonna take a quick shower," he said without turning.

The words were casual. But the door closing behind him felt like a curtain dropping.

I stayed in bed, staring at the ceiling, blanket tucked around me like armor.

Maybe I was imagining things. Maybe it wasn't weird. Maybe I was overthinking it.

But the truth sat heavy in my chest, unwelcome and unshakable.

It mattered.

And that scared me more than I wanted to admit.

GRANT

The water was too hot.

Or maybe I was trying to scald the confusion off my skin.

I braced my hands against the tile, let the spray pound down my back, and tried to believe it would help. It didn't.

All I could think about was Mia.

The way she smiled when she thought I was asleep. The way she kissed my chest like it was second nature. The way her voice caught when she said "unexpected island fling," like she needed me to laugh before she found out it wasn't funny.

She wasn't wrong. On paper, that's exactly what this was. Two strangers. A storm. A shared bungalow and a night neither of us had planned.

But it didn't *feel* like that.

It felt like something had shifted. Something real. Something I couldn't quantify or control.

And I didn't know what to do with it.

Because I don't do chaos. I don't do off-plan.

But Mia? She *was* chaos. Wild, brilliant, impossible to ignore.

And here I was—standing in the middle of it, soaked and stunned, already wondering what I'd do when it ended. When she left.

Because last night didn't feel temporary.

It felt like the start of something I didn't understand.

And that terrified me.

Because I didn't know if it was real to her, too—or if I was just a vacation story.

A knock at the door.

Soft. Hesitant.

Then: "Grant?"

I froze. Steam clung to my skin, thick and suffocating.

I wasn't ready. Not for her. Not for this.

But Mia had never waited for *ready*.

"I'm coming in," she said—and a beat later, the door opened just enough for her to slip inside.

"Okay," she started, arms crossed, eyes searching. "Here's the deal. I don't know what last night meant to you. I'm not trying to be dramatic, or slap labels on feelings that haven't even figured out their names yet."

She paused—breathed like she had to steady herself.

"But I know what it meant to me. And I need to know if I'm the only one who felt it."

The air changed.

"I didn't plan this," she went on, softer now. "I didn't come here looking for anyone. Especially not someone like you. But then you showed up—with your stormy eyes and your spreadsheets and that ridiculous jawline—"

I made a choked sound. She ignored it.

"I like you, Grant," she said. "In a way that's terrifying and weirdly honest. And maybe this was just a fling for you. Maybe you're already halfway out the mental door. But I need to know. Was it real? Or just... the storm?"

My chest was tight. My mind was chaos.

And still—I reached for her.

No logic. No hesitation. Just instinct.

I stepped out of the spray, water streaming down my body, and took her hand. She didn't flinch. Just looked up at me like she was bracing for the worst.

Instead, I pulled her forward—closer—until the water hit her too. Her breath caught.

"Mia," I said, my voice rough and low, "it's real."

Her eyes searched mine.

"I don't know what to do with it. I didn't expect this. I didn't want this. But it's real. You're in my head. You're under my skin. And I don't want it to stop."

Water slid down her face. Her lashes. Her lips.

She looked like a painting come to life. Too vivid. Too much.

Exactly what I needed.

"I came here to shut the world out," I whispered, my forehead resting against hers. "But you showed up. And now I don't want to go back to before."

She swallowed. "So it wasn't just the storm?"

I shook my head. "It was you."

Then I kissed her.

Slow. Certain. Like I already knew I'd never get enough.

She kissed me back with that same urgency, her hands in my hair, her body pressing close. I backed her against the tile, the heat between us sharper than the spray.

She gasped, then laughed—a low sound that wrecked me in the best way.

"Grant," she whispered.

I lifted her easily, her legs wrapping around me like they belonged there.

And then I was inside her—deep and sure and exactly where I wanted to be.

The heat was instant. The rhythm, instinct.

Her moans echoed in the steam as I moved, her fingers clutching my shoulders, her body arching to meet every thrust.

"God," she panted, head falling back against the wall, "this—"

I kissed her again, swallowing the rest of her words. Her cries. Her breath.

We didn't stop.

Didn't slow.

It was fast and hot and overwhelming—like something had been unleashed between us. A promise. A reckoning.

And when we came—together, hard—it felt like gravity broke and rebuilt itself around us.

We held on like we meant it.

And this time, I didn't wonder if she'd walk away.

I just held her tighter.

Because for the first time in longer than I could remember—I didn't want to be anywhere else.

Chapter Nine

GRANT

WHEN WE FINALLY STUMBLED out of the shower, soaked, unsteady, and more tangled than ever, I dried off with a towel too big for one person but just right for two. Mia laughed into the fabric, bright and breathless, like maybe everything would be fine—as long as we stayed exactly where we were.

"Wow," she said when we finally came up for air. "That was... thorough."

"Fast learner," I said with a grin that felt way too easy.

And for a moment, it was just that—easy.

No second thoughts. No exit strategies. Just two people who'd found something unexpected in the middle of a storm and decided not to let it go.

Then the lights flickered.

Once. Twice.

And then—on.

A low whir buzzed through the walls as power surged back into the bungalow. The fridge kicked on. A few forgotten lamps blinked back to life. And from somewhere behind me, Mia made a noise that could only be described as a *victorious squeak*.

"I have never loved electricity more," she said, holding the towel like a cape and marching triumphantly toward the bed.

I didn't even make it two steps after her before the phone rang.

We both froze.

Mia turned slowly, eyes wide. "If that's your secret bungalow girlfriend calling, now would be the time to mention it."

I rolled my eyes and turned to the landline. "This is Grant Ashford," I said as I picked up the phone. Then, I hit the speaker button and set the phone down so Mia could hear.

A pause. Then a voice—brisk, polite, and clearly running on hotel-concern autopilot—came through the speaker.

"Mr. Ashford, good morning. This is Lena from the front desk. We're calling to check in with all guests after the outage. Is everything alright at your location?"

"We're fine," I said, glancing at Mia, who was now dramatically draped across the bed like a Roman empress in a towel. "No issues."

"I'm delighted to hear that," Lena said, a note of relief in her voice. "While reviewing the registry this morning, we discovered that your bungalow was accidentally double-booked just before the storm. We sincerely apologize for the oversight. We've prepared a second bungalow and are ready to move one of you there immediately—of course, both vacations will be fully comped."

I glanced at Mia.

She arched a brow, then—without breaking eye contact—let her towel slip just enough off one shoulder to hint at all the reasons we didn't need two bungalows.

My throat went dry.

"Actually," I said quickly, turning back to the phone with the poise of a man barely hanging onto his sanity, "that won't be necessary. We're perfectly comfortable."

Mia bit her lip and gave me an innocent look that was anything but.

"Very well," the woman on the line said, sounding slightly confused. "If you change your mind at any point, please don't hesitate to—"

"Thanks, will do," I said, cutting her off with practiced corporate efficiency. "Have a great day."

Then I hung up.

MIA

Grant was still watching me. Barely holding it together. Which, honestly? Fair.

I adjusted my towel like it was a designer gown, struck a regal pose on the bed, and sweetly said, "Were you saying something about separate accommodations?"

He narrowed his eyes. "You're evil."

I beamed. "I know."

He sat down on the edge of the bed, quiet like the air had shifted.

"So," he said.

"So?" I echoed one brow lifting.

He let out a slow breath. "Now what?"

My stomach did a little flip.

"Like, existentially?" I asked. "Or are we talking about breakfast?"

He gave me a look. The kind that said *don't deflect this, Mia*.

I sobered. Just a little. "You mean now that the storm is over?"

He nodded.

I looked at him, really looked at him. Rumpled hair. That impossible jawline. The softest trace of uncertainty in eyes that had felt like home last night.

"Do you want there to be a 'now what'?" I asked.

His eyes didn't leave mine. "Yes."

My breath caught.

"I don't know what this is," he said. "I don't know what it turns into. But I know it doesn't feel over."

A smile tugged at the corner of my mouth. "Good. Because if you'd said 'thanks for the memories,' I was fully prepared to weaponize this towel."

He laughed—quiet and low like it slipped past his defenses. "Please don't. I'm not equipped for that kind of warfare."

I leaned in heart thudding. "Then let's figure it out."

He didn't answer right away. Just looked at me like he wasn't sure how this happened—how *we* happened. And honestly? I didn't know either. But I knew what I wanted.

So when he reached across the bed and took my hand, I let him.

"I want more than one storm," he said, voice rough.

My breath hitched.

And in that moment, something clicked into place. Not perfectly. Not neatly. But enough.

He was logic. I was chaos. But maybe—just maybe—we were figuring it out anyway.

Epilogue

MIA

Six months later…

The storm rolled in like déjà vu.

Thunder, low and steady. Rain streaked down the windows in frantic bursts. The city outside blurred into light and wet pavement—but in here, wrapped in Grant's arms, skin still warm from the shower and his breath steady against my neck, it felt like the calmest place in the world.

Lightning cracked across the sky, lighting up the room for one bright, heart-stopping beat.

I flinched.

He didn't.

He just tightened his hold—like he remembered exactly how to anchor me when the world got loud.

"I used to hate storms," I murmured, fingers tracing idle shapes across his chest. "They made me feel... unmoored. Like everything could fall apart at once. But now?"

I looked up at him, my heartbeat tapping wild against my ribs.

"Now I kinda like them. Maybe because I finally have something solid to hold on to."

Grant didn't smile. Didn't tease.

He just looked at me—like I'd said something far more profound than I meant it to be.

"I love you," he said quietly.

Like it wasn't a confession.

Like it was a fact.

Like gravity.

I blinked at him. "You can't just say that when I'm not emotionally braced for it."

He tilted his head slightly, lips twitching at the corners. "Seemed like the right time."

My throat went tight.

And for a second, I did what I always did—opened my mouth, ready to toss back something sarcastic. Deflect with humor. Keep it light.

But nothing came out.

Because I felt it too.

All of it. Crashing through me with the same reckless certainty that brought me to his bed in the middle of a tropical storm and never quite let me go.

"I love you," I whispered, eyes stinging. "God help me, I really do."

He smiled then—small, quiet, steady—and pulled me in like it was the easiest thing in the world.

Outside, the storm raged on.

But inside?

We were finally home.

***

Dear Reader,

Thank you so much for spending time with these stories—and for falling (just a little) for these billionaires right along with me.

Writing this series has been pure joy: the chaos, the chemistry, the complications..

. and the characters who somehow always find their way to love, even when they really shouldn't.

Whether you laughed, swooned, blushed, or bookmarked a favorite moment—thank you.

Your support means more than you know.

With love and caffeine,

Hana York

Hana York Books

Hearts on Duty Series

Sparks of Temptation

Love's Anchor

On Call for You

Investigating Desire

Falling for the Rescue

A Heart Worth Mending

***

Don't Fall for the Billionaire Series

Hating Mr. Wentworth

Tempting Mr. Dawson

Unraveling Mr. Ashford

For a full list of titles, please visit Hana York's website

www.HanaYork.com

About the Author

HANA YORK WRITES FAST-PACED, heart-pounding contemporary romance packed with irresistible heroes, strong heroines, laugh-out-loud banter, and just the right amount of spice to keep things sizzling. Her books are for readers who love grumpy men falling hard, fierce women who don't need saving, and the kind of chemistry that sparks off the page.

When she's not crafting stories full of love, tension, and toe-curling moments, you'll find her daydreaming about small-town charm, plotting ridiculous meet-cutes, and consuming an unhealthy amount of coffee. She believes in happily-ever-afters, overprotective heroes who don't stand a chance against their heroines, and that every great love story should come with a side of sass.

If you love forced proximity, off-limits attraction, sizzling tension, and romance that makes your heart race, welcome to the world of Hana York!

Follow Hana York for new releases, exclusive content, and behind-the-scenes fun! www.HanaYork.com

Find all her books here: https://www.amazon.com/author/hanayork

Follow her on Instagram: https://www.instagram.com/hanayorkromance/

Follow her on Facebook: https://www.facebook.com/hanayorkromance/

Follow her on Good Reads: https://www.goodreads.com/author/show/54826946.Hana_York

Join her mailing list here: https://www.hanayork.com/subscribe